The Cell Block Presents…

MOB$TAR MONEY
The Adventures of the Prodigal Son...

Published by: The Cell Block™

The Cell Block
P.O. Box 1025
Rancho Cordova, CA 95741

Facebook/thecellblock.net

Cover Design: Mike Enemigo

Send comments, reviews, interview and
business inquiries to: thecellblock.net@mail.com

Table of Contents

Chapter 1: How it all Started

"Tray, you're going to face some obstacles in life, but always remember, there's nothin' you can't overcome, 'cause God is always going to be your source of strength, and with God on your side, nothing can conquer you. Just keep your faith in Him. He'll never leave you, even if everyone else does..."

"Even you," Tray mumbled to himself as he sat thinking about his last conversation with his mother, who'd sat nodding and scratching until she bled as she tried to tell him how to overcome the obstacles he'll face in life. She repeatedly succumbed to her many obstacles, which were mainly heroin, as well as mentally and physically abusive men.

What's now been four and a half years seems like only yesterday since the night his mother and her boyfriend Terrell left him and his eight year old brother home alone while she supposedly made a quick run to the store.

Patiently, he waited for them to return so he could enjoy the pint of Cookies-N-Cream ice crème, which was his favorite, that his mother and Terrell had promised him for staying home and babysitting his little brother Damon.

Tray wasn't stupid. He already knew that Terrell, his mother's latest live-in thug of a boyfriend didn't like having to buy them things, but Tina, Tray's mom, had made it clear that her kids were part of the package when dealing with her. So Tray made it his duty to add to the list of expenses her boyfriends had to endure in order to enjoy alone time, and those that didn't want to pay were ran off ASAP!

After what seemed like an eternity, he and his little brother fell asleep on the couch, curled up, but were abruptly awaken by loud banging on the apartment door. At first, Tray thought the banging was coming from the TV, which was left on while they slept. Suddenly he could hear his mother screaming his name and telling him to open the door.

As he ran to the door and opened it, what he saw would be etched into his mind for as long as he lived. Tina and Terrell were covered in blood. Tina had blood pouring from gaping shoulder and leg wounds, and Terrell had been shot in the face and upper chest, blood was running down his track-infested arm, leaving the money he had clutched in his grip soaked in blood.

The neighbor from across the hall opened the door to see what the commotion was and was shocked at the sight of the two. Screaming for her boyfriend to call the police, she helped Tina and Terrell into their apartment and told Tray and Damon to go into her apartment and wait for her. They did as they were told.

That was the last time either Tray or Damon saw their mother face to face. Now their only communication was by letters or phone calls, and both were sporadic.

Tray was jarred from his thoughts by his grandmother's voice: "Tray, can you go to the store for me and grab a few things, baby?"

"Yes, ma'am. What do you need me to get?"

"Here. I wrote everything down for you. And here's twenty dollars; you can keep the change, baby," she said handing him the list and the money.

As he stepped out to go on the errand for his grandma Mabel, he couldn't help but think of how much he loved and appreciated her. She truly went out of her way to provide a better life for him and his little brother. She had been there for them since she found out about the night that his mother and her boyfriend tried to rob the liquor store and got shot up. Child Protective Services tried to step in, but grandma Mabel wasn't about to lose her only grandchildren to the California system. She had vowed to fight for them or die trying! In the end, she was granted full custody of Tray and Damon and they had been with her ever since.

As Tray walked past Sutter Street, his attention was drawn, like always, to the house with all kinds of cars and people in front of it. He always wondered who they were and what they were all doing there. One thing he noticed was that they were always wearing all the finest clothes, drove the cleanest whips and wore all kinds of jewelry. Every time he walked past, they seemed to be having a lot of fun. He wished that he could be a part of their crew, but he'd always been the shy type and had trouble initiating conversation with people. He was usually quiet and alone, and tended to fantasize about fun things he wished he could do.

Just as he was about to look away from the crew of people, he noticed one of the young dudes, who was about his age or so, was staring at him. As they both made eye contact, the young cat threw up the "Playboy Bunny"; Tray returned the gesture as he went on his way.

Shortly after stopping for his grandmother's items, he was coming out of the store when he realized Bango, the neighborhood bully who was 6'4" and 245 pounds, had arms as big as Tray's legs and a vicious set of hands – many grown men couldn't match him in hand-to-hand combat — was waiting for him.

"Hey, Tray! You got that five dollars?" he asked Tray. Now, Tray didn't owe him five dollars, Bango just charged him five dollars every time he saw him; the price to not get beat up.

"I-I-I don't got no-no money. Just my grandmother's money," Tray stammered. "I don't give a fuck whose money it is, nigga!" Bango yelled at Tray.

Just as Tray was debating if he should just give Bango the five dollars he said he owed him, "Bitch-ass nigga, you ain't gettin' shit," come from behind him. As Tray turned to see where the voice was coming from, he recognized the young cat that had thrown up the Playboy Bunny.

"Nigga, mind yo' bidness," Bango said less aggressively.

"Mark-ass nigga, this is my bidness! So take that strong-armin' shit somewhere else. This is the lil homie. You got a problem with him, you got a problem with me. If you got a problem with me," he said as he reached in his waist, pulled out a Glock .40 and cocked it, "you got a problem wit' MOB $tars!" He pointed the pistol at Bango.

"Nigga, do you know who I am?" Bango said as he tried to save face in front of the growing crowd.

"Who you are don't even matter. And I suggest you step lightly through these Central streets 'fore yo' homies be pourin' out liquor in remembrance of you. Now bounce!" he yelled as he let off six shots in the air, causing Bango to jog off while nervously looking over his shoulder. The crowd of onlookers started clapping because someone had finally stood up to the neighborhood bully.

"Hey, my boy, good lookin' out," Tray said to the youngsta with the fearless swag.

"Don't sweat it, bruh," he said as he turned around and introduced himself. "My name is Tyson, but everyone calls me Villian."

"What's up, Villian? My name is Tray, and everybody calls me that," he responded as the two shook hands.

"Where you from, Tray?" Villian asked curiously. He could tell by his demeanor that he wasn't from the central streets of Stockton.

4

"I'm from Sac, but my mom went to prison so I live with my grandma up the street."

"Well, my nigga, where you be seein' us all hangin' on the block, on Sutter Street, that's where I be. Come through and kick it wit' us sometime. Just ask for me," he said before going his separate way as Tray headed home.

Chapter 2: Delores

Tyson grew up an only child. Delores, his mom, had always worked hard to make sure he had everything he needed; name-brand clothes, all of his favorite foods, and even the newest electronics and gadgets. She gave him everything except the one thing she couldn't -- affection.

Delores had moved to Stockton after meeting a slick-talking older man who had promised her the world on a platinum platter, but instead had given her a Mason jar full of shit!

When she first met Slim, he was the nicest, sharpest, cutest and most attentive man she had ever met. She fell in love with him almost immediately. Every time she turned around, he was doing something to blow her mind. That all changed when he convinced her to come to Stockton with him. She first noticed the change when he would bring her around his family and friends. While they were alone, he would treat her as an equal, but around them he would distance himself and treat her like a child.

Finally one night she decided to confront him on it, while Slim and his cousin Sam Sneed, who'd always make sexual advances toward her while Slim just laughed, were smoking weed, snorting powder and kept bossing her around.

"You know what, Slim, fuck you!" she yelled at him, finally at her breaking point. "I'm tired of you always treating me like I ain't shit in front of your family. I'm going back to Oakland!"

"Bitch, you ain't goin' nowhere but in that muthafuckin' kitchen to cook," Slim said as he and Sam started laughing at her for throwing a temper tantrum.

"Yeah, OK, nigga, I'ma cook yo' ass somethin' alright. I'ma cook yo' ass some grits!" she said, referring to when Al Green had hot grits thrown on him.

Slim understood the threat behind her comment and said, "Keep on; yo' mouth is gonna get yo' ass *whupped*."

"Whatever, nigga. That's all you know how to say is --"

That was as far as she got. All she remembered was him turning in her direction, and the next she knew she was waking up with Sam zipping his pants up. As she tried to clear her thoughts and remember what had happened, she realized that her skirt was up around her waist and her panties were torn off of her.

As the reality of what had happened to her had set in, so did the realization that she truly had to get away from him. When she called her dad in Oakland and explained what had happened, he responded with; 'That's what happens to little whores who want to chase after every nigga with a slick mouthpiece and sells 'em a dream', before hanging up in her face. With nowhere else to turn, she did whatever she had to do to make it. To add insult to injury, she soon found out she was pregnant.

She vowed to be strong, keep her baby, and make sure its life would be better than hers. She also made a promise to never trust another man, and she never did. This is why she had a very hard time showing affection even to her own son, though she definitely did her best.

Life was all good until she got this big job opportunity working for a major pharmaceutical company as a general manager. It had been fifteen years since she walked out of

Slick's life and she'd never looked back. Sure, she had suffered a couple of struggles and setbacks, but for the most part she couldn't complain, and she did it all without a man in her life. She owed her success to nobody and nothing but her hard work ethics, her determination to provide for her and her son, and the grace, mercy, and guidance of God.

So when she was presented with this huge opportunity she knew it was a major blessing. The hours were longer and the drive was farther, but the pay was practically double what she'd been making before. After only a few days on the new job, she became friendly with a lady named Cristi who was always fun to work around and easy to get along with, and besides, they both stayed in the same neighborhood. So they agreed to share a ride to work to save money on gas. Everything was going well until one night Cristi invited Delores over for a little get-together. At first Delores was hesitant, but finally decided: What the hell, it's Friday. I don't have to work tomorrow and I haven't enjoyed a good party in quite some time.

After getting cleaned up and changing clothes, she gave Tyson, her son, money for him to go to the movies with his friends, then left to go meet Cristi.

After meeting up, Cristi said they had a couple things to pick up. First they stopped at Delta Liquors to pick up some Paul Mason, Hennessey, and a couple of Jack Daniels wine coolers. Next they went to the south to buy some bomb. While sitting in the car wash parking lot, listening to Lil Wayne's song Lollipop while Delores watched Cristi try with all her might to make her flat ass bounce to the music, suddenly a purple and chromed-out "Box" Chev Caprice pulled up with its music so loud and full of bass, you couldn't even hear Lil Wayne in her car, and the entire ground of the carwash vibrated tremendously.

Once the car was pulled up beside them, Cristi went and hopped in the passenger seat. Within seconds she hopped back out, came back to her car and they drove off.

As she reached into her pocket and came out with a half-ounce of bomb, the air was permeated with the powerful scent of the weed.

"That nigga got it bad for me, girl," Cristi said. "Every time he sees me, he practically begs me to eat the pussy. I might just let him if he keep actin' right."

"That nigga look like he can have any bitch he want," Delores said, thinking to herself, this bitch is so full of herself. See, Cristi was a white girl on the outside, but as black and hood as ever on the inside.

"Yeah, he probably can have any bitch, but he don't want 'any' bitch, he wants the baddest bitch" she said as she laughed at her own joke. "Can you blame him?" she said, causing Delores to laugh at her as well.

After they got back to Christi's spot, everyone began to arrive and they were all introduced to Delores.

As the night progressed and everyone was well intoxicated, Cristi came out with two more blunts and fired them up. Delores had just passed the blunt after hitting it a few times when she noticed the euphoric feeling coming over her and she started sweating profusely. She thought that maybe it was because she had drank so much because she wasn't a big drinker. But when she hit the blunt again, that's when she noticed the smell of the blunt was different, and she noticed everyone's eyes were glassy and they were all sweaty, too.

Going to find Cristi, she pulled her to the side. "Bitch, what's in this weed?" Delores asked her.

"The shit's good, huh?"

"What is it?" Delores repeated herself and shook Cristi by the shoulders.

"Damn, bitch, calm down! It ain't but a lil cream."

Delores, not being up on all the street terminology said, "What the fuck is cream?"

"It's crack," she said as she laughed at the expression on Delores' face.

"Bitch, I don't smoke crack!" Delores yelled at Cristi

with a look of irritation on her face. "What are you tryna do, turn me into a crackhead?"

"Damn, Delores, I'm sorry. I didn't mean to offend you, I just wanted to show you a good time, girl. Please forgive me OK?" Cristi pleaded with her.

"OK, girl. But you should let people know before you try to give them something like that, you feel me?"

"Yeah, I feel you. So, what; you didn't like the shit?" Cristi asked.

"I guess it was alright. Why, you got some more?" Delores asked.

"Yep. I'll be right back," Cristi said as she ran upstairs.

While Delores waited for her to return, she got the weirdest feeling that she had just stepped onto a road of no return.

Chapter 3: Tyson

Tyson was posted on the block with his crew thinking about the cat Tray he had met earlier at the store. He reminded Tyson of himself; when life's circumstances had thrust him into the street life to fend for himself in a desperate attempt to find a respectable identity. In some strange way, he felt the need to help Tray find an identity that wouldn't allow him to be a victim to predators like Bango.

Tyson was in Tray's shoes less than a year ago. He came home from the mall one day expecting to see his mom in the kitchen cooking dinner, but instead he saw her on the floor searching for crack crumbs.

At first he didn't know what she was doing, but then he spotted the small mirror with the crack rocks and razor blade sitting beside a crack pipe.

Tyson had a friend named Steelo who sold crack. Occasionally Tyson would hang out at Steelo's dope spot. You could always count on getting a few good laughs while watching the crackheads' actions due to the effects of the drug. But seeing his mother in this mind state was far from a laughing matter.

He tried to help her sober up by hiding her crack from

11

her, but she became violent and tried to attack him. Hurt and confused, he gave it back to her, locked himself in his room and left her alone.

About an hour later, he was just about to go spend the night at his friend's house when there was a loud scream, and then a BANG!, CRASH!, and the sound of glass shattering. Tyson ran from his room to see what was going on; his mom was on the floor, shaking, with glass all around her from the glass table she fell through while clutching her chest.

Rushing to her side and calling 911 at the same time, he tried to console her as tears flooded his eyes. He suddenly found himself saying a prayer, asking God to save his mom. But before he could finish, he heard his mom take a deep breath. As she reached and grabbed his arm, her eyes had widened and she whispered, "I'm sorry, baby." As her eyes closed, she released the grip on his arm, along with her last breath.

When the paramedics arrived, they tried to revive her but it was too late.

For two weeks he tried to clear his conscience of the guilt he felt for not putting up enough of a fight with his mom over the drugs. He wandered the streets day and night with in destination in mind. He wore the same clothes day after day and hardly ate anything. Then one day he ran into an older cat named Drak who'd been seeing him around the hood. Lately he'd seen that Tyson looked a little rough and lost, so he decided to see what his situation was.

As Tyson was walking down Harding Way, the smell from the burrito truck had his stomach growling like two pit bulls fighting over a bitch in heat.

Just when he was thinking about how bad he wanted something to eat, he heard, "Hey, lil homie. You want something to eat?"

Tyson thought to himself that God must have read his mind.

"Yeah," Tyson answered him, but was a bit hesitant in

approaching the man.

"Hey, with the rest of that change, let the lil homie order what he wants," he said to the lady in the taco truck. After Tyson finished getting the food and the change he told the guy thank you.

"Don't even trip, lil homie. What's your name?" he asked.

After thinking to himself that he hoped this ain't no fag shit he said, "My name's Tyson."

"Well, my name is Drak. Come on, let's roll for a minute," Drak said as he hit the alarm on his Chrysler 300. "Hop in."

Once inside he noticed there were TV screens in the dashboard and a fold-down screen in the roof. When Drak started the car, videos started playing on the screens. As he was engrossed in a Mozzy video, they pulled up onto Sutter Street and parked.

After turning the car off, Drak turned to Tyson: "So, lil homie, now that you got some food in your stomach, talk to me. What's goin' on with you?"

"What do you mean?" Tyson replied.

"I mean, why are you walkin' around lookin' lost, wearin' the same clothes all week, and took the risk of gettin' in a car with someone you don't know? That's what I mean, lil bruh." As Drak saw the expression on Tyson's face he said, "You ain't gotta be ashamed, but what's goin' on, dog?"

"I just lost my mom. She OD'd smokin' crack," Tyson said as his eyes started to tear up. "She was all the family I had."

"Where are you staying?" he asked him.

"Nowhere. I spend the night here and there, but mainly I just walk around."

"Well, as long as I'm around, you ain't got no worries, feel me?"

"Alright, big dog," Tyson said.

That was almost a year ago and he hadn't looked back

since. Drak turned out to be the leader of a notorious crew of young criminals called the MOB $tars. They consisted of jack artists, drug dealers, pimps and prostitutes, gun runners and murderers. To top it all off, Drak was a dirty undercover Narcotics Task Force agent. He was born and raised in East Palo Alto and was lucky enough to make it out the hood, but the hood had never made it out of him.

He used to work deep undercover drug operations. His job was to get inside and bring down major drug dealers, drug runners, and organizations. He was good at what he did and played his role so well because he was so hood oriented. He was held in the highest regards, until one day a major mistake had cost him an informant's life. He was severely reprimanded and suspended without pay pending investigation. This is when he created his MOB $tars organization.

Eventually he was called back to active duty on the force, but there was one problem: The seed for financial greed had already taken root and it was an unstoppable force. He vowed to take over the central streets of Stockton one block at a time, and he was doing his thang to make that happen.

Chapter 4: Welcome to the Hood

As Tray was buying the Black and Mild cigar from the corner store, he found himself wondering if Villian was over at the Sutter Street spot. He decided to slide through to see if he was there.

As he left the store and was waiting for the light to change, he heard, "What you got in yo' pockets, homie!' Tray stiffened and turned slowly, then he heard Villian bust out laughing.

"Nigga, you was spooked to death. Unclench yo' ass cheeks, dog. You safe." He started laughing again then stuck his hand out; "What's up, lil bruh, why you ain't stopped by the spot yet?"

"Actually, I was just about to come through now," Tray said, shaking Villian's hand, relieved it wasn't Bango.

"Come on then. I got some shit for you anyway, my nigga," he said as he and Tray took a shortcut to the spot. As they climbed a fence into the back yard, Villian took his Glock .40 out from under his velour Polo shirt and slid it inside a slot that was attached to a garage. Suddenly the slot slid open and a hand reached out, retrieving the handgun.

"There're no weapons allowed inside the spot, only outside. Inside all is well, and we one big family. No need for weapons. Come on," Tyson said as walked into the back entrance of the house, up the stairs and into a long hallway.

Coming to a door marked "The Lab", Tyson opened the door and turned the lights on.

As they entered the room, Tray spotted a sexy, chocolate, thick-ass bitch laying in the bed with the covers hanging halfway off of her, pleasuring herself while watching a porno. She kept doing her thang like they weren't even there.

Tray stared with his mouth open until Tyson got his attention; "Oh, yeah, that's the homegirl Mona. She stay poppin' X and watchin' porn. Hey, Mona, this is my boy Tray 8," he said, introducing the two.

As Mona took one of her hands from under the blanket, she waved and said, "What's up, lil daddy?" then went back to doing her thang.

"Come on," Tyson said, leading Tray to the closet. When he opened the door it was like walking into a department store. His clothes closet was on deck. Tyson said, "Pick you out four outfits, Playboy. The shoes are over here and the jackets are over there."

"Nigga, is you serious?!" Tray said excitedly. "This is all top-of-the-line shit!"

"I know, nigga. We don't half-step 'round here, bruh. We do it big. But let's take one step at a time," Tyson said as he watched Tray look around like a kid in a candy store. "Go 'head!"

As Tray picked out clothes, Tyson went and dug in a drawer and came back. "Find you some shit, I'ma run downstairs for a minute," he said before leaving.

As Tray was about to try on the Red Monkey jeans, he felt a presence behind him. When he turned around, he saw it was Mona; standing there with a seductive look on her face and lust in her eyes. Walking towards him, she put her finger to her lips; "Shhhhhh."

Suddenly she pushed him down into the chair that was next to a large full-body mirror. Unzipping his jeans, she pulled him out, and in one swift motion engulfed his whole package. Immediately swept up in an intense wave of pleasure, he grabbed a fist full of hair and moved it out of the way so he could see her putting in work. He noticed that she was just as interested in watching as she was watching herself in the full-length mirror. Just when Tray thought it couldn't get any better, she jumped on top of his lap and straddled her legs over the arms of the chair, grabbed him beside his head and shoulder and raised herself up and down on top of him until he couldn't take it any longer and busted off inside her tightness. As they both came together she kept saying, "This my dick! This my dick! This my dick!" until they both collapsed against each other.

As she got up off his lap, she kissed him on the cheek, gave him a wink, and left as silently as she came. She returned shortly later and gave Tray a wet soapy rag; "Go 'head and clean up. When you're dressed, Villian is waiting downstairs." Then she left.

After getting dressed and inspecting himself in the mirror, Tray went downstairs to find Tyson. As he stepped into the spacious living room, he spotted Tyson sitting next to a sexy, exotic, caramel-skinned Puerto Rican broad. She had long silky braids that flowed down to the middle of her back. Around her forehead she had a bandana that said MOB $tars. She was Villian's girl and her name was Blaze.

"What's up, lil bruh? Glad you could join us. Everybody, this is Tray 8," he said as everybody nodded in his direction. "Come on, have a seat," he said to Tray.

When Tray sat down, Tyson stood up, walked to the center of the room and gave a quick rundown on how he'd met Tray. He also told the crew how Tray had reminded him a lot of himself.

Suddenly he turned to Tray and said, "We are one big family. We all have similar backgrounds and we all share the same goal; to get money!" Suddenly they all threw up the MOB hand sign. "We feel like we can help you by bringing you into our fold -- our family. We're winners; and as long as you wit' us, you'll be winnin' too. So tell me; you ready to shine like a star?"

As Tray thought about the opportunity that was in front of him, he thought about how just last week he was wishing he could be a part of their crew. Funny how things happen.

"Yeah, bruh, I'm in," Tray said. Then he was embraced by each member, Tyson lastly.

"Welcome home, family. Welcome to the hood. Now, by me sponsoring you, you are my "off breed". Anything you do comes back on me, so make me proud, dog." Tyson reached into his back pocket and came out with a diamond-encrusted link chain. Hanging from the chain was a medallion of a large star with the words MOB $tar going through it. He walked over to Tray and put it around his neck. "With this chain, you become a link in the echelon chain that holds this organization together. We are all equal and are only as strong as our weakest link. So we give each other strength until death separates us; MOB!" he said loudly before everyone followed with 'as one!'

Unfolding the same bandana Blaze had on her head, he placed it around Tray's head and said; "With this flag, you pledge to put Money Over Bullshit for as long as you're linked to this committee. With that said; MOB!"

"As one!" the crew followed.

Easy as that, Tray had dedicated his life to the MOB $tars crime family. He finally felt a part of something, and he was ready to prove his loyalty.

Chapter 5: Blood Oath

Later that night Villian and Tray were sharing a blunt. Tray didn't really smoke much, but he didn't want to seem like a square around his new family so went on and got with it. He'd also drank a Red Bull and Hennessey mix, so he was feeling nice.

"See that nigga in the black Sean John warmup suit? That's Trigga Dave. He and his bitch, "Cripani", run guns all
up and down the highway, and they own the club Passions," Villian said to Tray. "Oh, and the bitch Mona that gave you the warm welcoming," he said with a knowing smile on his face as Tray realized Villian had set that up. "She's our best-kept secret. We use her to bait niggas to their doom. Don't let her sexy looks fool you; that bitch got 6 bodies under her belt."

"Damn! I wouldn't wanna cross her," Tray said with a smile on his face.

With a very serious look in his eyes Villian said, "I wouldn't either, 'cause the bitch like karma; if you got somethin' comin', she'll make sure you get it."

Villian suddenly reached into the bushes and pulled out a chrome 9mm, racked a shell into the chamber, stuck it into the small of his back and said, "Come on. We gotta go handle some bidness."

As they crossed the street, Villian came out his pocket with the keys to a black Monte Carlo Super Sport on black and chrome 22 inch rims. Starting the car with the remote, the music immediately came to life with bass pounding so hard it shook the concrete and rattled the nearby neighbors' windows. The two climbed in, buckled up, and punched out leaving a cloud of smoke as the tires tried to grip the street.

"In these streets, you have to have respect, bruh. If you don't have respect, you'll never be able to establish any position of power. Sometimes, the only way to get respect is to take it," he said as he pulled the car over next to an apartment building and told Tray to follow him. While they walked towards the building, Villian was talking to someone on his Bluetooth earpiece. As they got to the entrance, Villian suddenly turned to Tray, pulled out the 9 from his waist and said, "You ready to take yo' respect, Tray 8?" as he held the pistol out to him.

"Yeah, what you want me to do?" Tray asked enthusiastically.

"Face your fear," he said, opening the hallway door and leading the way.

In the near distance Tray heard a whining voice say "What I do to y'all? Come on, man, I got kids that need me." As they came around the steps, Tray immediately recognized the voice; it was Bango!

"You remember my lil homie Tray 8" Villian asked Bango.

Bango, seeing Tray with the gat in his hand started trying to plead with him; "Tray? What's up, big homie?" he said like he was glad to see him again. "I see you done finally came up, man. That's hella cool."

"Nigga shut yo' mark-ass up! Nigga the other day you was on some big bad wolf shit. Now you damn near wanna suck his dick. Get on yo' knees, nigga," Villian said as Bango did as he was told.

"So, what's it gonna be, dog? There's yo' respect. Are you gonna take what's yours?" Villian said and turned to Tray.

As Tray stood before the few members of his new family, he knew his loyalty and courage was being tested. This may be the only chance to prove himself, so he went all out.

"Empty yo' pockets, bitch nigga!" Tray said to Bango.

"Man, I only got a few dollars to buy my lil son some Pampers," Bango pleaded.

"Mark-ass nigga, I don't give a fuck who or what it's for; tear it off!" Tray said, remembering all of the five dollar bills he had given Bango.

As he started to reach into his pocket, he tried to make a dash for the door, but Tray was faster and he clipped him as he ran past. The sweat that was pouring down Bango's face and chest, combined with the forward momentum of him trying to break out running like Marion Jones; as soon as he hit the floor, he slid all the way to the door on his stomach. They immediately started stomping him.

"Ah! Aaahhh! I'm sorry! I panicked! AAAHHH!" Bango screamed and pleaded.

Suddenly Tray stepped up, reached down, grabbed Bango by the braids and shot him in the back of the head: BOOM! Blood splattered from the force of the impact caused by the Rhino sluggs that penetrated both skull and concrete before landing itself into the apartment floor. Placing the 9mm into his waistband and walking out the door, Tray never looked back.

As Villian and Tray drove off, Tray sat in a daze. His ears rang as he thought to himself, I killed a man. Looking into the side view mirror, he realized he had specs of blood on his face. He wiped his face off, fired up a Black and Mild, and laid back, closing his eyes....

When he opened his eyes back up, they were parking in front of the house.

"You know, lil bruh, you made me proud. I knew you

were ready. You faced your fear tonight. As long as we know you're brave enough to stand alone, you'll never stand alone. We move as one," Villian said. "Now you're official; 'cause, see, its blood in, blood out. In order to show your commitment to us, there has to be bloodshed. So that's what tonight was about."

"But what if I hadn't killed Bango?" Tray asked.

"Remember when I said we're only as strong as our weakest link?"

"Yeah."

"Well, that would've been seen as weakness. Always remember; the weakest link is the first to be replaced," he said as he looked Tray in the eyes. The meaning of his statement was loud and clear to Tray.

Later that night, after leaving the crew, Tray took the necklace off and wrapped it in the bandana, then placed them both inside his jacket pocket. As soon as he walked into the house his little brother said, "Dang, Tray; where you get those new clothes at, bro?" causing his grandma Mabel to glance up from her nightly crossword puzzle and inspect his new attire.

"I got a new job working with my friend and his dad at their clothing store. He gave me some stuff for the cleaning we did at their other store today. Don't trip, lil bro, you know I'ma get you some clothes, too. You know why?" Tray asked Damon.

"Cause you love me just as much as Jesus do," Damon said, giving Tray a high five and a hug.

Walking over to his grandma Mabel, he bent over and kissed her on the cheek. "And I can't forget the most special woman in my life," he added as he hugged her tightly and said, "I love you, grandma."

"I love you, too, baby. Supper is on the stove. Don't forget to pray before you eat, OK?" his grandma reminded him.

Grandma Mabel felt a strange spirit around Tray when he came home, but he'd never given her any reason to

22

doubt his integrity. He'd always been honest with her, so she said a silent prayer over him asking for God's protection and guidance, then went back to her crossword puzzle.

As Tray enjoyed his dinner, he kept thinking of the day's events. He couldn't believe he was a part of the MOB $tars, and on top of that, he had a body under his belt. His life was finally about to have some excitement!

With a smile on his face, he went back to his meal, still thinking about his luck.

NARCOTICS...
DRUGS...
OWN...
UNDER...COVER...

Chapter 6: Agent Jones, AKA Drak

The two detectives stood in the parking lot of the Stockton Police Department sharing information while they smoked a cigarette. Suddenly a cocaine-white Challenger with a midnight-blue padded top, Gucci crocodile interior, sitting on 24-inch blades came speeding up into the parking lot with the music pounding so hard that several car alarms started screaming. When he parked and stepped from the car, the platinum Rolex watch and chain was shining so hard you had to squint in order to look directly at them; not to mention the diamonds on every finger, except his pinkies, which had two rings apiece. He was decked out in a sky blue North Carolina jersey, LRG jeans, and a pair of sky blue Timberlands. On his waist were two phones; one for his personal use, the other for business. To the average person he looked like any other drug peddler. But to the Stockton Police Department, he was one of their own. He was Agent Jones, an undercover Narc.

As he walked past the two detectives in the parking lot, the look of jealousy and envy were written all over their faces.

"While motherfuckers like us have to work our asses off just to try to make ends meet, you got niggers like him

24

beep boppin' around with their pants hanging off their asses and having all the money," said the white detective to his partner.

Once the two finished their smokes, they entered the building and asked the receptionist to show them to Captain Moody's office. The receptionist led them to the Captain's office and said, "Wait right here, I'll let him know you're waiting," as she knocked on the door and entered the office. After only seconds she returned; "The Captain will see you. Right this way."

When the two stepped into the office the Captain stood to greet them: "I'm Captain Moody, and this is Special Agent Jones of our Narcotics Task Force," he said as he reached out to shake their hands.

Feeling dumb about the nigger comment he made earlier, the detective realized that who he thought was a common drug dealer was actually one of their own, working undercover.

Shaking the Captain's hand, then turning to shake Agent Jones' hand he said to him: "So, you're Special Agent Jones. I've heard a great deal about you, sir," feeling the need to stroke the man's ego after racially profiling him earlier.   RACIALLY...

"I hope it's all been good," Agent Jones said with a smile on his face.

"Yes, it's all been good."

"We hear you're one of the best in the field," his partner said, cutting him off. "I'm detective King, and this is my partner Detective Howard," Detective King said as he shook Agent Jones' hand.

After everyone was situated, Captain Moody said, " I was just filling Agent Jones in on what's going on, but you can start fresh."

"Well, we have information that a major drug distributor is forcing a warehouse owner and his wife to allow him and his crew to store large quantities of dope in their place of business. They have showed us pictures and they swear that they are not in on the drug operation. They have been sworn to secrecy, and the men have a list of their family members' names, addresses and social security numbers. They also said that if anybody contacted the authorities, or if anything happened to the drugs, the whole family would be exterminated," Detective King said, then looked to see if he had their undivided attention before continuing. "Now, they pick up the drugs every month at 12:00 am on the first, and drop more off at 12:00 am on the fifteenth. The husband works late on Friday nights; something to do with inventory. We can meet up with him on the Friday before this upcoming first of the month. We'll set up surveillance and make other arrangements to secure these people."

As they finished up, Agent Jones paid special attention to the warehouse on the photo that was being passed around. Little did the agents know he didn't have to study the photo; it was one of his spots, where he stored the product sold through his drug organization. Mr. and Mrs. Baker, I warned you, he thought to himself.

After they wrapped everything up, Agent Jones immediately hopped into his whip, fired up the powerful engine and smashed off to Sutter Street.

Villian and Tray were sitting on the hood of the car listening to the new Mozzy CD when Villian's girlfriend, Blaze, came and handed him his phone. "It's Drak," she said as she started to playfully slap box with Tray.

"What's up, lil rogue?" Drak said in his deep voice.

"What's up, Drak? What's good, big bruh?" Villian returned.

"I heard you finally got you an off-breed, bruh," Drak said, sounding proud of his protégé. "Have you tested him yet?"

"Come on, big bruh, you know I'm laced by the best. You insultin' my character," Villian said as he started laughing because he knew Drak was very proud of him.

"My bad, lil bruh. Well, I might have a mission for y'all

26

tonight. I'ma need you to let Mona and Blaze know that tonight is they night to shine. Plus, I'ma need a few of y'all to move some hardware for me tomorrow. So be ready, 'cause this is real urgent. Now, put Blaze on so I can let her know what's goin' down— MOB!"

"As one," Villian responded before giving the phone to Blaze.

Grabbing the phone, Blaze walked off as Drak laced her game up for the mission.

"Ey, dog, we got another mission tonight so I'ma need you to have ya mind right," Villian said to Tray. "This will fa sho put a couple dead presidents in ya pocket. How ya love that?"

"Fa sho, I'm lovin' that. I'm always up to get money. What we got to do?" he asked Villian curiously.

"Hold on, lil Flash Gordon. When the time's right, you'll know everything, but right now, you got bigger issues to handle, dog," he said to Tray with a smirk on his face.

Seeing that Villian was aware of something he wasn't, he became really intrigued: "What you talkin' 'bout, homie?" Tray asked. But as he noticed Villian watching behind him, he turned around and spotted Mona. She was baby-oiled up, hair freshly braided and her make-up was flawless. She was rockin' a pink, plaid, Gucci mini dress that came to the middle of her creamy thighs, and a white button-down short-sleeve blouse buttoned at the bottom of her ample cleavage with the ends tied in a knot above her navel that held a diamond-encrusted Playboy bunny. She knew that she was the shit, and it was time that Tray recognized.

"Nigga, is that how you fuckin' wit' it? Get what you want and don't even holla at a bitch?" she said with her arms folded and braids all over the place trying to keep up with her neck movements. This only added to her beauty. Tray had never had a broad jock his swag like that, so he really turnt it up.

27

"Damn, lil mama. Is that how *you* fuckin' wit' it? I mean, you fine and all that, and you rockin' the fuck out that outfit, but what's the use in wearin' it if you gonna throw yo' sweatsuit on?" As he got within arm's reach, he wrapped his arms around her, palmed her ass, gently nibbled on her bottom lip and whispered in her ear; "Save all the sweatin' for the sack, with yo' sexy ass."

"You lucky you turned yo' charm on, 'cause I was about to give yo' ass the bizniss!" she said as she grabbed his chain and pulled him in for another tender kiss. After a couple seconds, Tray had to come up for air or risk drowning in her passion from a lack of oxygen.

"We better save this for later; 'fore I take yo' ass upstairs and give yo' ass the bidness!" Tray said with his hands still palmed on her ass.

As she turned to walk away, she stopped and lifted her skirt up, sat it on top of her bodacious ass, made it bounce and said, "You got the talkin' part down to a science, but you gonna need more than some slick talk to show me, lil pimpin'."

As everybody cheered Mona on and laughed at Tray, he stood stunned. He knew that he would never live it down if he let her leave on that note, so reaching into the small of his back, he pulled the 10mm out, slid it into the bushes, then went and handled that. He couldn't allow his new fam, or anyone, to think he would back down from anything!

GIAS... OUT.. CAR...
CLOTHES... OFF.. BACKS...
OUT.. MOUTHS.
TAKING... FOOD
SELLING... BRICKS.
INTO.. EAR... BUSINESS.. TURF...
WHISPER

Chapter 7: Puttin' in Work

BLOCK

After enjoying several hours of relaxation, it was time to get down to business. Mona and Blaze dressed in their hooker attire, then came downstairs as everyone gave them their appraisal. "These niggas ain't ready," Blaze said, giving Mona a high five and a sisterly hug; "MOB!" she said into her ear.

"As one," Mona whispered back.

"Let's get this meeting going," said Drak as the crew gave him their undivided attention. "First, I'd like to welcome the newest of the breed, Tray 8. Next, we have to put down a demo. It seems that we got a couple cats from Oakland that've been sellin' weight on MOB turf. So that means they takin' food out our mouths, clothes off our backs, and gas out our whips. This means we gonna have to give them a much-deserved 'Welcome to the MOB', ya dig? Now, this is how it's gonna go down..."

OUNCES.. **$$$$$**

As G-Rock and Philthy posted on the block, they felt good about the night. They'd brought four bricks of powder coke and four ounces of heroin from their Oakland connect.

DRUGS... COKE.. HEROIN...

They had already sold one whole brick of powder and an eighth of the second, and cats were still sliding through to cop the cheapest ounces of potent coke since the early eighties, thanks to their Columbian connection. They'd been coming to Stockton for about three months and the money was lovely.

They had heard of the MOB $tars and that this was supposedly their turf, but they were determined to keep getting this easy money, and fuck who didn't approve of it; if they had problems, they could handle it like gangstas.

As they passed the blunt and bottle of Hennessey back and forth, they saw a black Monte Carlo Super Sport on black and chrome 22s turn the corner and park. As the two cats got out of the car, G-Rock and Philthy spotted the bangers tucked in their waist. They could tell that they were young, but they had the look in their eyes of men who had lived long and seen a few things. As they passed, they noticed the chains that they wore were expensive and had stars with the word MOB in the center.

When the pair entered the corner store, G-Rock and Philthy dismissed them and went back to drinking and smoking.

"Girl, ain't none of these limp-dick niggas out here got no stamina," said a thick-ass Puerto Rican chick with long braids and a banging ass body.

"I know that's right, bitch. I get more nuts off solo bolo than I do with these can't-fuck-ass niggas 'round here. Plus, I can go all night and ain't gotta hear a bunch of, 'Hold on a minute. I need to rejuvenate'." The girls busted up at the comment. "Rejuvenate from what, nigga? You ain't done shit!" They continued to laugh.

"Damn, y'all jus' walkin' 'round verbally bashin' niggas, huh?" Philthy asked the thick-ass Puerto Rican chick.

"Umm, excuse me, but do I know you?" Blaze asked with much attitude.

"Naw, not yet. But you sho can get to. My name is Philthy and this my boy G-Rock. We got major stamina and dick for days; what it do?" he asked while giving them an extra-long glimpse of his gold grill.

Not at all impressed with his game or his gold grill, she decided to play into his lame rap. "Well, Philthy, my name is Blaze, and this is my homegirl Mona. Now, you talk a good game, but a pair of lips will say anything to get what they want, sweety," she said as she leaned up against their black and gold BMW 750 sedan with the brains blew out, sittin' on BBS rims. "Now, if yo' dick as big as yo' mouth, then you might get to go a couple rounds in this platinum pussy. How you love that, papi?" she added as she lifted up her skirt and gave them a glimpse of her freshly shaved pussy; Mona stuck her finger in her mouth, got it nice and wet, pulled it out to show them how wet it was, then reached over and rubbed it back and forth over Blaze's slit while Blaze moaned softly. That was all it took; like a sheep led to the slaughter house, they were hooked.

Just as they were about to drive off, cars came from everywhere. Niggas were jumping out with masks on telling the driver to turn the car off. With a car in front of them and a white Challenger behind them, Philthy came to the harsh reality that there was no escaping. As he watched his side view mirror, he spotted an officer walking toward him with his badge dangling from his necklace and a smirk on his face.

"Officer, what's going on?" Philthy said with both of his sweaty palms clutching the steering wheel.

"Well, first of all, you're contributing to the delinquency of a minor. Now, step out the car, nice and slow." Obeying the officer, everyone exited the car, placed their hands on the hood and were searched.

"What are you guys up to? You wouldn't be out here selling drugs, would you now?" Drak asked them.

"Naw, we were just talking to these girls, officer," G-Rock said, sweating profusely.

"You mind if I check the vehicle, sir?" Drak asked Philthy.

Then one of the cats who was playing the role of a cop said, "We got some dope," as he held up a large bundle of dope and reached for Philthy's wrists.

"Man, that shit ain't mine," he said. "That's bullshit! You planted that on me!" He tried to turn around, but was swept off his feet and slammed into the curb. With blood leaking from his mouth, he said, "What the fuck is goin' on?"

"What's goin' on is, you better never act like you want to raise your hand to an officer of the law. This time you got off with a busted grill, next time I'ma bust a cap in yo' ass. Now, my boss said, do you mind if he searches the vehicle?"

"I ain't got no choice, do I?"

"Not really. But you ain't too good with choices no way, 'cause it was a real stupid choice to peddle yo' dope in Stockton." He turned to his partner and said, "Go ahead and search it."

No sooner than the trunk was opened, Drak pulled out a duffle bag containing two bricks of powder, wrapped; several bagged-up ounces of powder; four ounces of heroin; about $17,000 in bundles and an electronic scale.

"Let me guess: he planted this on you, too; huh, goldie?" Drak said with a smirk on his face. "Now, all of this dope, and the contributing to these under age prostitutes; with those kinds of charges, you'll be doin' a whole lot of squattin', coughin', and guardin' yo' booty, 'cause anything to do with you fuckin' with minors isn't something you want to let yo' celly find out about. Now, you was mentioning choices, so I got a couple for you; you can either jump in your car and hit the highway, or you can take your chances with the San Joaquin Municipal Courts. If I was you, I would choose wisely."

"Man, keep that shit! Let us go, we'll never come back to Stockton," G-Rock said without having to waste any time thinking about it.

"Then bounce!" Drak told them.

As the two got into their car and damn near wrecked trying to get off the block, Villian and Tray, who had been watching the corners, yelled out, "Coast clear, let's roll!" Everyone jumped in their whips and smashed off, heading to Sutter Street.

When they all made it back to the spot, everyone was still charged up from all the action. Tray was especially exhilarated. He felt like he hadn't truly been living until now. He was part of an entity that had respect and feared nothing. He had a beautiful woman, more money than he ever had ($5,000 was his share), and a new-found way of seeing life in general. He felt there was nothing he couldn't attain.

Later that night, after calling his grandma Mabel and getting permission to stay out, he sat around with a few of the older MOB $tars.

Mack was another sharp individual. He was married to a sexy-ass Haitian chick named Roxy, who had long silky dreadlocks and spoke with a thick exotic accent. She also had the sexiest green eyes Tray had ever seen. She was bisexual, very attracted to Blaze, and didn't hide the fact. Now, Mack also owned a strip club called The Chop Shop; bitches had bodies of every make and model and everything had a price. And everything meant just that — everything! Mack also sold jewelry, and could literally get his hands on just about everything because his family owned several pawn shops from Stockton to the Bay Area.

"So, what you gonna do with that money you made tonight, Tray 8?" Mack asked, trying to see where Tray's mind was at as far as knowing how to utilize money.

"Well, first thing I'ma do is put half in the bank and let that draw interest. Then I wanna get my lil bro some clothes to make him feel good, and plus I wanna get my grandma somethin' nice," Tray said, hoping it was the right thing in front of the OGsS.

"That sounds like a cool lil start-up plan, but we make real power moves and we get major paper. That shit you came up on today? Peanuts to an elephant, lil bruh. If you wanna elevate in this world, it starts with elevatin' how you think. If you think small, your lifestyle will reflect it. See, people who are really broke need for others to see them as bigger than they truly are. But when you truly playin' wit' paper, the only person you should want to impress is you. Let the broke niggas break they pockets tryna live beyond they means, while you sit back and stack ya chips up like a can of Pringles."

As Tray took all of the wisdom in, he couldn't help but feel the love he'd craved from his mother being manifested before his very own eyes from his crew. It was surreal to him.

"When you ready to really get ya paper up, lil bruh, let me know and I'll teach you how to invest your money in stocks and bonds. You wanna see some real money, invest in some oil, or even some kind of computer technology," Mack added as he and Roxy got up to depart. "Don't forget the mission we got in the morning," Mack reminded him. "Drak said to make sure everyone is where they 'posed to be at the appointed time and not a minute later. MOB!"

"As one," they all responded.

Chapter 8: Quality Time

After everyone went to enjoy some quality time with their mates, Mona and Tray followed suit. When they got up to the room, Tray noticed it had been rearranged. There was a huge partition that had been set up to separate the bedroom into two separate living quarters. On her side was exotic hues of orange, lime green and pinks. Everything was neat and in its own special order.

"Welcome to my sanctuary," Mona said, softly but full of excitement. "I see you changed everything around."

"Yeah, when you first seen it, I didn't have any reason to fix it up, but now..." her voice trailed off as she looked around bashfully.

Turned on by this shy side of her, he reached and wrapped his arm around her waist, nuzzled her gently, then softly nibbled her earlobe and neck. As she started to melt into the contours of his sensual embrace, suddenly she stopped him, stepped back and said, "Let's slow down, pimpin', cause we need to talk. But, first..." she went to her drawer and came back with a sack of chronic and a Hennessey blunt wrap. "Will you do the honors?" she asked, handing him the items.

While Tray started to break up the chronic, he saw

Mona fumble with a container. After taking something out she said, "Lift up your tongue." After seeing the look of confusion on his face, she smiled and said, "What, you don't trust me? Or are you just scared?" And just like that, she got him to rise to her challenge. As he lifted his tongue, she placed a pill in his mouth and said, "Let it dissolve under your tongue."

Now, Tray wasn't stupid. He'd seen others pop X, but he'd never tried it. He heard it's supposed to be a euphoric feeling, but little did he know, he was in for an experience he wouldn't soon forget.

Tray had just finished firing up the blunt when Mona said, "So, Tray, what's up with me and you, daddio? You know I'm feelin' you, have been since I first seen you, but you haven't told me what's on your mind yet. So tonight is yo' night to open up."

"What do you wanna know?" Tray asked as he blew out a huge cloud of smoke and started to cough.

After he got his composure, he looked at her with glossy eyes and a smile on his face. He started laughing at the facial expression she was making.

"Boy, don't play wit' me, you know what I mean. Now what's up?"

Passing her the blunt he said, "OK, baby girl. Yeah, I'm feelin' you somethin' crucial, and I can see us doin' this long-term, but how do I know where your loyalty lies? 'Cause I ain't tryna play no games; I left those alone in junior high school, feel me?"

"I feel the same way. Look, I won't lie. In the past I've broken a few promises and hurt a few hearts, but only 'cause people would continually hurt me," she said with a hurt look on her face. "My own mother killed herself and left me and my lil sister with nothin'. So, yeah, I've endured some pain in my life, but I've also experienced happiness. It's been a while since I have, but I know happiness when I'm experiencing it, and, Tray, I'm experiencing it with you," Mona said, looking Tray directly in his eyes before hitting the blunt and passing it back to him.

Tray didn't know if it was the effects from the ecstasy pill and chronic concoction, or if he was just hypnotized and intoxicated by her unique beauty and conversation. One thing for sure, he didn't want the feeling to end. As he reached and put the blunt out, all at once their lips connected and the two became one. Slowly they undressed each other without their lips ever separating.

Taking one of her breasts into his mouth and running his tongue around the nipple, a wave of pleasure exploded inside of her and a moan escaped from her throat -- "aahhh." As he heard the affect he was having on her he was thoroughly excited. Just when he thought he was in control of the situation, the stakes were raised tremendously as Mona flipped him over onto his back, straddled his chest backwards and backed her pussy up to where he had full action to eat at her buffet. As she grinded herself on his face and stroked him to full erection, he felt a pair of lips slide down his penis while she continued to stroke him. As he opened his eyes, he looked up and saw Mona caught up in the pleasure he was giving her with his tongue while she looked over her shoulder at him. Confused, but still enjoying the mysterious blow job, he looked around Mona to see who had him in their best of interest, and was stunned when he saw Blaze deep throating him while Villian beat it up from the back. When he saw that Villian was in on the ordeal, he relaxed and floated away in the cloud of ecstasy.

Chapter 9: The Setup

When Tray woke up the next morning and rolled over, Mona was sitting Indian-style, watching him and putting makeup on.

"Wake up, sleepy head," she said with a smile on her naturally beautiful face. "I got your things set out and your shower stuff ready. Make it quick. We only have an hour and a half to be in position, so chop chop."

As Tray bent over to pick up his boxers, she smacked him on his ass playfully; "Where's my good morning kiss?" she asked.

Reaching for her braids, he grabbed a handful and pulled her in; "Good morning, my love," he said as he walked into the restroom to get ready.

About twenty minutes later, he emerged looking like a million bucks and some change. He walked into a cloud of smoke as Mona and Blaze sat giggling and smoking the first blunt of the day.

"What's up, GQ smooth?" Blaze said as he walked into the room.

"What up?" he said with a huge grin on his face still unable to believe he'd had his first ménage a trios. As both girls giggled, Blaze continued to tease him; "So, how was your night?"

Tray reached for the blunt, took a puff and said, "It was alright," with a smirk on his face.

"Yeah, we heard the fuck outta that. Nigga, you loved every minute of that shit and you know it," Blaze said as they busted up laughing and high-fiving each other. Tray couldn't help but join in on the laughter as Mona kept demonstrating his facial expressions from the night before.

"Y'all leave my lil nigga alone," Villian said as he walked in with a huge smirk on his face. Then he, too, started demonstrating Tray's facial expressions along with them, causing Tray to bust out laughing even harder at their antics. "Naw, seriously; you ready, nigga? We gots to handle our bidness," Villian said as he hit the blunt.

"I'm ready, let's roll," Tray said as he slid on his stunna shades and strolled off with major bounce in his swag.

After retrieving their weapons and saying their good-byes, they hopped in their separate whips and went to their destinations.

At 11:00 the crew pulled up into Baker's Automotive Warehouse. Mr. Baker came out in hopes of making a sale as it had been days since he last sold an automobile; he had bills to pay and was beginning to get desperate. So at the sight of the Monte Carlo Super Sport, he figured these were some individuals that didn't mind spending money.

As he was walking towards the car, he suddenly heard fast-approaching footsteps. Just as he turned to see what was coming, he spotted a black canvas sack being pulled over his head.

"Mr. Baker, just cooperate and everything will be alright. If not, you and Mrs. Baker will be a memory. Do I make myself clear?" asked the voice. Mr. Baker shook his head in compliance.

"Now, we're gonna go for a ride; but remember, if you cooperate, you'll live.

As Mr. Baker was taken around back and placed in the trunk of a luxury sedan, the men set out to retrieve the narcotics and replace them with boxes identical to the original ones that the narcotics were stored in. After replacing all of the boxes, Blaze and Roxy, dressed in Fed-X uniforms, jumped in the van, drove it to the designated location and waited for further instructions.

Back at the warehouse, Villian and Tray were taking apart the dashboard of Mr. Baker's Mercedes and hiding a kilo of dope, cut down and bagged up into ounces, inside. Under the seat they stashed a paper bag with 12 ounces and in his trunk they hid another paper bag of money containing $4,600 and a quarter ounce of heroin. After everything was set, Tray and Villian jumped in the whip and went to put the second part of the plan into motion.

$$$$$

While Mrs. Baker stood in her yard watering the garden, two young men in overalls and tool belts pulled up and got out.

"Hello, Mrs. Baker. We're here to restore your central air system. Your husband Tom asked us to stop by."

"I didn't know it needed restoring, but come along. I hope you can find everything, 'cause I don't know the first thing about where to find all those thingamajigs," she said as she let them inside. After a couple of minutes of watching them set up, Mrs. Baker lost interest and said, "Would you fellas like something to drink?"

"No, we're fine, ma'am," Tray said.

"Well, if you need me, I'll be out front watering my garden," she said as she left them to the job.

As soon as she left, Villian pulled out the chrome 9mm and went in search of the couple's bedroom. When he found it, he slid the murder weapon used to kill Bango underneath the mattress and left the room. After sliding a slip of paper containing Bango's name, address, and an amount of money to be paid the day before his death into the tablet beside their telephone, Tray and Villian packed up and left.

40

"I hope you fellas found everything all right," Mrs. Baker said.

"Yeah, it was no problem. Tell Tom that we'll send him our bill, and you have a nice day, Mrs. Baker," Tray said as they pulled off and jumped onto the highway on the way to meet up with Blaze and Roxy.

After everything was set up, the crew back at the warehouse let Mr. Baker out of the trunk, unharmed. Now, Mr. Baker, we appreciate your cooperation. And it would be wise of you to forget we were ever here," said the voice.

"No problem, sir!" Mr. Baker said with excitement in his voice. "But if you don't mind me asking, what's all this about?"

"We mind! Now, we want you to come to Lincoln Park tonight at 8:00. That gives you a chance to close down the warehouse and meet up with the boss. Is that clear?" the voice asked.

"Yeah," he said very nervously.

"Look; don't trip. If I wanted to hurt you, you would have been hurt already. So I'll see you at 8:00 tonight, right?"

"Sure, I'll be there," Mr. Baker said, relieved.

$$$$$

"Where can I report a homicide?" Mona asked as she popped her gum repeatedly.

As the receptionist looked up from her paperwork, she spotted Mona standing with her hands on her hips, tapping her foot, and staring in her direction. "Yeah, have a seat. Someone will be with you shortly," she said before getting up to go get her some assistance.

After waiting for five minutes, Captain Moody came out and introduced himself; "Captain Moody, ma'am. I understand that you have some information for us?" he said to her.

"Yeah, but not right here," Mona said while looking

around nervously.

"Follow me; right this way, ma'am," Captain Moody said as he led her to his office. "Can I get you something to drink?" he asked.

"Yeah, a soda will be cool," she answered as she looked around his office.

Shortly after returning from getting her soda, Captain Moody and Homicide Detective Brad Coleman walked into the office.

"Here you go, ma'am," Captain Moody said as he sat the soda on a coaster in front of her. "This is Brad Coleman from our homicide division," he said as Detective Coleman extended his hand to shake hers.

"Hi," she said as she shook his hand limply; she has a deeply ingrained dislike for officers of the law.

"Can I ask your name, ma'am?" the detective asked.

"Yes. My name is Kelisha Davis," she said, giving her alias.

"OK, now, what is this about a homicide?" he asked her.

"It's about Terrell Hopkins, they call him Bango. He's the one who was killed in the Madison Arms Projects last week. All last week, a white man in a silver Mercedes kept coming to look for him, and he had a chrome gun. He kept telling me Bango had messed up his dope money, and he wasn't gonna accept any loss on his money. He was either going to pay him in cash, or blood. He even said anyone who would help him find Bango would be paid for their tine," she said, quoting the script that Drak had told her to report.

"Do you know if anyone took him seriously?" he asked her.

"I don't know. I tried to warn him, but Bango kept telling me, 'Fuck that faggot. I'll pay him when I get his money'. Then, the night he was killed, I heard the gunshot and saw the same white man walk out of the building with the gun in his hand. As he jumped into his Mercedes, I

42

copied down his license plate numbers," she said, reaching in her purse.

Not able to believe his incredible luck, Detective Coleman's smile lit up the office as he waited for her to find the numbers to the license plate.

"Here it goes; P-8-4-0-D-F-K," she said, handing the paper to the smiling detective.

"Mrs. Davis, thank you for the information. We'll be getting in touch with you."

"Hold on; ain't no reward or nothin'?"

"Is that why you offered this info; 'cause you're lookin' to get paid?" he said.

"No, I'm doin' this because he didn't deserve to die. Now his daughter has to grow up without a daddy, like half the girls in our neighborhood. So we want justice. But I got bills, too; so don't get it twisted, Mr. Detective."

"OK, OK. I didn't mean to offend you, Ms. Davis. Look, this is how it goes; if your information leads to an arrest and a conviction, then we'll contact you about a possible reward," he said.

"Alright," she said as she picked up a pen and paper, wrote a fake address down and got up to leave. "I'll be lookin' forward to hearing from y'all," she added as she left the office. Thoroughly satisfied with her performance at deceiving the detective, she left the police station and went to go meet up with her crew.

As soon as she pulled up at the designated meet spot, Drak and Mack pulled up and parked behind Villian and Tray. As Blaze and Roxy climbed out the van, they came over to Drak's Challenger.

"Well done, $tars. Everything is in place. Mr. Baker isn't gonna know what happened. Now, Blaze, I still need you to drive the van to Sacramento. We got a trap spot we're gonna house the hardware and product, but you're gonna have to be careful 'cause the projects you're goin' to ain't no joke. It's the Franklin Villa apartments, better known as G-Parkway. I'm gonna have you trailed by Tray 8 and Villian to make sure you're secure, but still; you have to get in and get out. Now, Mona, I'm gonna need you to stay in the lead of the pack by at least a half a mile. That way you can alert the crew to any kind of threat ahead. Does everyone understand their positions?" Drak asked everyone. They all nodded in agreement.

"Well, alright; with that said, be safe, and we'll meet up later. MOB!"

"As one!" the crew responded. Then they departed and headed toward the highway.

Chapter 10: The Sting

After leaving the crew, Drak made his way to the Stockton Police Department. As he made his way to the Captain's office, he spotted Detective King and Detective Howard sitting in the office, engaged in a conversation with Captain Moody.

When Drak knocked lightly on the door, Captain Moody waved for him to enter.

"Agent Jones, you're just who I need to see. You're not gonna believe the luck we've had," the Captain said. "Try me," Agent Jones said.

"Well, first, we had an eyewitness come in and give us crucial information into the murder investigation of Terrell Hopkins. Full detail, including a license number and make of a car. I ran the license number by DMV and the Mercedes came back to none other than Tom Baker of 11673 Country Club Boulevard. She said that he had been coming around looking for the victim for a couple days and offering rewards for his whereabouts, and that the victim owed him a bunch of money for drugs. The bastard's a dopeman and a murderer. He lied about the whole 'being forced to hold the drugs' bit."

"I bet he was gonna take a large quantity, set up the

connect for the fall and keep all the money. All the while, he's portraying himself to be the victim. You gotta admit, he's clever. He almost outsmarted us," said Agent Jones.

"Well, I'm gonna nail his ass to the wall. He's gonna wish that he'd never seen drugs or guns when I'm through with his fucking ass.

"Well, actually, it gets even sweeter. Today I ran across one of my informants who personally buys dope from Mr. Baker in bulk. He actually has a deal set up, meant to go down tonight at 8:00, in Lincoln Park. I even read his text messages to my informant. He's supposed to bring us a kilo," Agent Jones said as he thought about him and Mack texting back and forth. Only, Drak was texting Mack from Mr. Baker's phone, while Mr. Baker was riding in the dark trunk. They had set up a buy for the kilo, and the text messages would for sure seal Mr. Baker's fate....

"Well, when he shows up to do the deal, we'll be waitin' for his ass with the K9 and a search warrant," Detective Howard said. "So let's set this shit up."

$$$$$

"I'm gettin' off at the Florin Road exit, and the cops are on my ass. Well, one cop, so I should be able to handle it. Y'all just pull over, and I'll let you know when the coast is clear," Mona said to the crew who was trailing at a comfortable distance.

Just as Mona cocked a round into the chamber of a double-action Smith & Wesson fourteen-shot 9mm, the officer who had his flashers on stepped out of his cruiser with a smile on his face as he walked towards her car. Suddenly Mona recognized his face; it was Big Red, a guy she used to date. He had once pulled her over in a stolen IROC-Z convertible, and instead of taking her to jail had asked her out on a date. They had a nice time, but again, her issue with law enforcement wouldn't allow them to become an item.

46

"Driver; cut the engine off, place your hands on the steering wheel and remain in the vehicle," he said with a huge, sexy grin on his face; he could tell that she recognized him from the expression on her face in her side-view mirror.

Mona put the 9mm under her seat and slid her skirt all the way up around her waist, giving her an eye-full of her creamy chocolate thighs, then she placed her hands on the steering wheel.

When Big Red got to the door, Mona acted as if this was her first time ever setting eyes on him.

"Well, hello there, sexy," she said as she started fanning herself. "You have to excuse me, Mr. Officer of the law. There's something about a man in uniform that gets me all hot," she added as she wiped her forehead, her cleavage, and then seductively rubbed away imaginary sweat from her creamy exposed thighs.

Big Red, thoroughly hypnotized, totally forgot about where he was as he grabbed his crotch, remembering the night he almost got to sample her goods.

"Why didn't you tell me you were going to change your number?" he said as he continued to look at her rubbing her thighs.

"I was in a bad place at the time. But I'm single now, so, what's up? You still wanna beat me up with that nightstick, sexy?" she said as she blatantly eyeballed his crotch, reached into her console, grabbed her pen, wrote a number down and kissed the paper leaving her lipstick impression, then passed it to him. "Call me Friday. And, oh, yeah; I need you to do me a favor," she added.

"Anything," he said obligingly.

"I need you to escort me to G Parkway, but first let me make a call," she said as she called the crew and told them that all was well and she had them a police escort!

After the business was handled and the crew was headed back to Stockton, only then did they all finally call Mona and congratulate her on the quick thinking and incredible luck, which earned her the baddest bitch crown.

$$$$$

Tom Baker had just closed the warehouse for the night, climbed into his Mercedes and was headed to the hood; Lincoln Park, crackhead heaven. A direct order was made for him to be there, which was his only reason for going. It was 7:45 pm, and that left him fifteen minutes to get there. Jumping on the highway, he saved a lot of time. He was just pulling up and parking, when suddenly police cars came rushing from everywhere and a police helicopter shined a light from the sky.

"Driver, kill the engine and exit the vehicle very slowly with your hands interlocked behind your head.... Now, lay face down on the ground, and do not move," an officer said who was pointing a gun directly at him with shaky hands.

As Mr. Baker followed instructions, he was handcuffed, placed in the back of a cruiser and read his Miranda rights. After being asked if he understood them, the officers asked for permission to search his vehicle, which he gratefully agreed to before being locked in the back of a cruiser.

While watching the K9 run through the back seat and then the front, silence was followed by the dog's loud yaps as it began to go crazy over something in the car. Watching from the cruiser, Mr. Baker was thoroughly confused. As an officer looked into a paper bag, he placed it on top of the car. After going back into the car, suddenly the officer said, "Well, take a look at what we have here." He held up a large duct-taped bundle, then looked in Mr. Baker's direction and shook his head.

Suddenly, another officer who'd been searching the trunk said, "We have more," as he dumped several bundles of money and drugs from another paper bag.

As Mr. Baker thought back to the events from earlier that day, he realized he'd been set up. He couldn't think of any reason why someone would go through such lengths to do this to him, and he vowed to get to the bottom of this whole mix-up.

$$$$$

At the same time that Mr. Baker's car was being searched, another search warrant was executed on his home, where police uncovered the murder weapon, as well as the address of the victim.

After being transported to the San Joaquin County Jail, Mr. Baker was booked in on first-degree murder charges, possession of an illegal firearm and aggravated drug trafficking. And, of course, transporting narcotics was an automatic ground to have your car seized. He was given a no-bail bond, because by him being from and having ties to another country, he was considered an extreme flight risk.

He was stuck like Chuck in a barrel of bad luck.

Chapter 11: Sitting on Top of the World

After only four months of being a member of the MOB $tars crew, Tray was touching more money than he'd ever thought imaginable. He had a sizable amount in the bank; he was investing in bonds; and he'd even invested in Mack's jewelry business, all thanks to Mack teaching him the importance of the almighty dollar. The good thing about investments are that you don't have to do the work. You just sit back and watch your money make you more money. But the key word is watch, because Tray had been taught to trust nobody completely. Nobody!

Even though Tray and Mona were still an item, they were starting to argue a lot. So, after a week of hard hustling and partying Friday and Saturday, he decided to go to church with his grandma Mabel, who'd practically been begging him to start back attending. So Sunday morning, Tray found himself sitting in front of Pastor Safford, whose message seemed to be directed at him, and, therefore, he had his undivided attention.

"...See, that's what's wrong with the youth of today. They want what they want when they want it and will go to any length to get it because Satan has put such an allure on these things. Now, when you combine this with the fact that most of our youth is growing up in a single-parent household, lacking any direction and guidance, there's no wonder why they find outside influences to be attractive to their young minds. See, what we need to start ins-tilling into them at an early age is that true value should come with a relationship from God, and what He gives you the ability to possess inside; not from if you have attained the things the world considers as valuable. See, instead of breakin' your neck and jeopardizin' your integrity to acquire the things your heart desires, God says to seek Him and His kingdom and His righteousness first, then He will give you the desires of your heart... We have to start resisting the temptations of the devil. And until you do, you will not gain the victory that is already yours, just yet to be claimed. Because greater is He that is in you, than he that is in the world...."

After service, everyone was preparing to leave. Many were talking and visiting amongst each other. Tray and Grandma Mabel were about to leave when they were approached by Mrs. Daisy.

"Hello, Mabel; hello, Tray," she said.

"Hello, Mrs. Daisy," they both said in unison.

"Tray, it was nice to see you. Hopefully we can see more of you. You know I'm in charge of the Young Adults Ministry. We could really use someone like you to reach some of the younger youth, as the Pastor was saying. So, what do you say, Tray?" she asked him.

"Well, I enjoyed the Pastor's sermon, so I'll definitely be back. Now, as far as the Young Adults Ministry goes, I'll have to think on it because I have to work," he lied.

"Well, there isn't a rush. When you decide, let Mabel know and she'll let me know. Now, Mabel, don't forget I'm throwing a barbecue next weekend. You all are more than welcome to come, OK? God bless you both," she said as she turned and walked away with the speed of a woman half her age.

As Tray and his grandma Mabel were walking down

the steps, he was bumped by a high-yellow, curvaceous, bow-legged cutie with freckles, dimples, and the sexiest little gap between her two sparkling front teeth.

"Oh! I'm sorry," she said as she gently wrapped her arm around his bicep to steady herself.

"No, you're sexy. And don't trip, you can bump into me anytime, lil mama," he said with a huge smile on his face and a twinkle in his eyes as he spotted her cheeks start to blush. "Oops, I didn't mean to make you blush, but I do admit, it does look beautiful on you," he said, causing her to laugh.

"Oh, so you just got all of the lines, huh?" she asked as she continued to grin.

"I wouldn't say that, but it's not an everyday occurrence that I bump into someone as beautiful as you are. And since this experience is so rare, I felt I needed to take advantage of such a precious moment while you're still a vision in my present rather than a missed opportunity in my memory," he said, turning his charm up to the max.

"Oh, yeah, you're good," she said as she took notice of his thick lips, silky eyelashes and dimpled cheeks, all accentuated by his immaculate razor-lined edge-up. Catching herself taking a visual inventory of his looks and build, she had to make herself stop. The pain from her recent loss was too great and fresh on her mind to even consider a new chapter in her life; especially with someone so suave and debonair as him. She could already tell that he was a heartbreak waiting to happen, and God was still healing her so she decided she had to pass on this opportunity.

"You know, you're real charming. Thank you for all the compliments, but, I'm really facing some obstacles in my life right now. Maybe another time, though," she said as she kissed her palm, placed it on his cheek, then turned and walked away.

"Well, can I at least have your name?" he asked with a hint of disappointment in his voice.

"Desire," she said before continuing on her way.

"Well, my name is Tray," he said; but it was too late, she had already went through the doors.

As he ran to catch up with his grandma Mabel, he couldn't help but smile to himself; he could see she was tempted, but at the very last minute had fled like he was the devil. He vowed to make it his duty to find out more about his new attraction: Desire.

$$$$$

Later that day, Tray came to the spot with a look of exhilaration about himself and everyone noticed it. "Damn, Tray 8, give us some of what you're on," said Villian, causing everyone to start chuckling.

"Aw, man, I went to the house of the Lord—"

"Ahh, man, don't tell me you done seen the light," Villian said, cutting him off.

"Naw, I didn't say that. Matter of fact, don't trip, y'all wouldn't understand anyway," Tray said, then reached for the blunt of Kush that was being passed around.

"Man, I'm sorry. I didn't know you had turned into Frank Sinatra," Villian said, passing the blunt.

"What's that supposed to mean, dog?" Tray asked curiously.

Suddenly the crew started singing: "Quit playing with feelings... Nothing more than feelings," as everyone burst out laughing.

"Man, fuck y'all!" Tray said before he started to laugh with everyone else.

"Let's go get some drank," Villian said he walked towards his car. "Tray, here you go; you're driving," he said, tossing him the keys.

As they jumped in the Monte Carlo Villian said, "Head to Conway, I got something I need to pick up. Oh, yeah; what happened at church?" he asked curiously as Tray jumped on the highway.

53

Looking at him to see if he was still playing or not, he said, "Man, it was like the pastor was talkin' to me. It was weird."

"That was the Holy Spirit ministering to you," Villian said. Thoroughly stunned, Tray couldn't believe his ears.

"What, you're surprised I know about the Lord?" Villian asked him. "My boy, I've spent a lot of time in church. I just lost my way when I lost my mom. I felt like God had let me down. It's really a long story. I'll tell you sometime," he said as he saw they were pulling into the Conway Homes. As he told Tray where to go, they suddenly pulled up in front of a yard with numerous cars parked out front. "I'll be right back," he said as he climbed out and was met by an older gentleman. After the two spoke, Villian jumped into a Cadillac CTS on 24s and told Tray to follow him.

As they pulled up into the liquor store parking lot, Villian got out and asked Tray how much he liked the CTS while they both admired the car.

"You already know I'm lovin' this. This bitch is clean," Tray said with a look of envy.

"Don't trip, you'll have something like this soon, lil bruh," Villian said with a smile on his face. "There's still a little work to be done to it; you ain't seen nothin' yet, my boy."

After they left the liquor store and dropped the car back off, they headed back to the spot to enjoy the rest of their day off and plan for the next upcoming meeting.

Chapter 12: Desire

As Desire and her son Noah were down on their knees praying, a single tear left a warm trail behind as it slid down her cheek, followed by another.

"Dear Heavenly Father, me and my son Noah come humbly before you, asking that you please have mercy on Terrell's soul. I know he wasn't righteous or perfect, but he made us happy. Please, allow him into your pearly gates, on our behalf, so we can one day spend some time with him, once Jesus returns, and please help me to continue to provide for my son and his grandmother. I ask of you, and thank you, in Jesus' mighty name, amen," Desire and Noah both said together at the end.

As Noah looked up at his mother, he reached up and wiped her eyes with his little hands.

"Don't cry, mama. We'll see him when Jesus comes back. And besides, you still got me, and I love you, OK?" Noah said.

Laughing at Noah and his innocence, she wrapped her arms around him, gave him a big hug and kiss and said, "And mama loves you, too, my lil king." They both kissed their palms and placed it on the tombstone that read 'In Loving Memory of Terrell Hopkins, 1995-2013, May he

Rest in Peace,' before getting up and leaving.

After doing some minor shopping, she and Noah made their way home to Mrs. Daisy's. She had been staying with her ever since Terrell's demise. At first, Desire had put up an argument, but Mrs. Daisy wasn't having it. Her and Desire had always been close. So, she wanted her and her great-grandson to live with her and Desire had eventually given in. On one hand it was good because Mrs. Daisy wouldn't let her pay any rent, so she saved money; but, on the other hand, everything in the house had reminded her of Terrell. This was making her grieving process a lot harder than she'd hoped it to be, but God was getting her through it.

"Oh, there you guys are. I have chili and garlic bread on the stove. Don't eat too much, 'cause we're having peach cobbler with vanilla ice cream on top for desert," Mrs. Daisy said.

"Yaaaaaaay!" Noah cheered. "Thanks, grandma Daisy! That's my favorite!" he said as he ran and gave her a hug.

As she hugged him back she said, "I know, so go wash your hands while I warm you up a plate, baby."

"Thank you, Mrs. Daisy. You truly are the best. We love you so very much. I don't know what we would do without you," Desire said as she gave Mrs. Daisy a hug as well.

"Believe me, I need y'all just as much as y'all need me. I couldn't stand being in this home alone," she said with a sad look in her eyes. "Come on, let's feed the little one," she added before going into the kitchen.

"Later, I'll help you start preparing for the barbecue tomorrow," Desire said.

"I already have everything set. You just get the baby's clothes ready."

"Alright," Desire said as she set the table for dinner.

Later that night, after putting Noah to bed, Desire lay in bed and thought about the time Terrell had saved her from almost being killed...

She had been walking home from school with her friend Spicy when they decided to stop at McDonald's on Charter Way. While they were in the line ordering their food, the gangbangers were behind them. Suddenly, Desire felt one of them rub his crotch against her ass. Turning around swiftly, she slapped the closest one to her and shoved him in the chest.

"What the fuck is wrong with you, bitch!" he yelled in her face.

"Bitch-ass nigga; what the fuck is wrong with you! Puttin' yo' dick all on my ass. You better keep it off my ass 'fore I cut it off. Then you can have it back to use as a straw to drink yo' soda wit', nigga!" she said as she pointed in his face. "Let's go!" she said to Spicy, who obeyed as the entire restaurant exploded into laughter at the two gangbangers left standing there looking stupid.

Just as the girls made it to the bus stop, up walked Terrell who was in Desire's math class.

"Damn, Desire, you really got off into that nigga's ass, lil mama," he said.

"What's up?" she said, still with a scowl on her face.

"Don't be mad at me," he said. Then he took his straw out of his soda, held it up and said, "Besides, I like this straw just fine," as they all fell out laughing.

Just when Terrell had mustered up the nerve to ask Desire for her number, a car pulled up and rolled its window down. The gangbanger stuck his arm out the window with a .380 clutched in his grip and yelled, "Hey, smart-mouth bitch!" then pulled the trigger twice in rapid succession; Terrell stepped in front of her and took a bullet in the arm, another in the pectoral muscle of his chest.

As the car sped off, Terrell collapsed to the ground, and both Desire and Spicy screamed, then knelt beside Terrell and cuddled his head. Suddenly, a grin appeared on his face.

"Calm down, ladies, I'm all right; I'm invincible," he said, right before he passed out.

The doctors said that by Terrell's muscles being so well-built, that the impact from such a small caliber weapon didn't do much damage other than some deep scarring. But just the fact that Terrell was willing to jump in front of a bullet to save her was a lot to be grateful for. So from then on, they were inseparable.

Well, at least until...

As she got Noah's clothes together, she kept thinking how long it had been since she'd even felt a spark of life. That had all changed within seconds of bumping into Tray last Sunday. She had found herself daydreaming about him often since that day. She didn't know when, she didn't know where; but one thing for sure, she couldn't wait to see him again. She thought of him that night as she lay down to sleep and she dozed off with a huge smile on her freckled face.

$$$$$

As Tray and his little brother were running around trying to add the finishing touches to their new outfits, Tray thought to himself what excuse he would come up with to leave the barbecue early. He was sure it would be dull and boring, full of old church people talking about the Lord and preaching to him, so he figured he'd come up with an exit plan before they even got there.

As soon as they got to Mrs. Daisy's street, you could hear music loud and clear. No sooner than when they started to climb the steps, Mrs. Daisy opened the door.

"Come on, y'all. Tray, you and Damon can head out back and join the festivities. Mabel, I need your help," she said, racing back to the kitchen.

When Tray stepped outside, he was astonished by all of the activities goin on. There were jumpers for the kids, a DJ booth, a booth for face painting; there were different games and contests.

Tray was fixing himself a plate when someone bumped

into him from behind.

"Excuse me, I'm so sorry. I am such a klutz," she was saying when the gentleman turned around and she recognized who it was. She laughed at the situation she was in.

"I'm starting to think this is how you pick up on guys, lil mama," he said with a smile on his face.

"Boy, shut up," she said playfully as she lightly pushed him with one hand, and held her son's hand in the other, continuing to laugh.

"And who is this lil fella," Tray said to the small child.

"My name is Noah; I'm four," he said while holding up four fingers on one hand and trying to pull his other hand free from his mother's grip. "Can I have some chicken, please?"

"You sure can, come on," Tray said as he reached for the child's hand. Once Desire released his other hand, Tray said, "My name is Tray."

"Hi, Tray. Do you like my mommy?" he asked curiously.

"Noah! Boy, if you don't mind your manners and quit bein' so nosy... I'm sorry, Tray," she said laughing at her son's boldness.

"I'm sorry, mama. I just want you happy again," he said as he looked at her sadly before turning to Tray; "Thank you for the chicken," he said as he hugged Tray's leg and ran off towards the jumpers.

"If I didn't know any better, I would swear you two set that up," Tray said and started laughing.

"That lil boy is a handful," she said as she laughed with him.

"I bet he gets it from his gorgeous mama," Tray said as he looked deep into her hazel eyes, causing her to look away. "Here I came to this barbecue thinking of an exit plan, 'cause I thought it was gonna be packed with old ladies praising and hallelujahing in Jesus' name."

"Naw, that's inside," she said as they both fell out

laughing. "So, Tray, how did you become so good with kids? Do you have any?"

"No, but I guess because me and my lil brother Damon are so close. Our mother went to prison almost five years ago. Even before then, she would leave us at home alone. So I practically raised him myself," Tray replied softly.

"Aaawwww, that's so sweet," she teased him playfully as he started to blush.

"Now it's my turn; what's your story? Last week you told me you were facing some obstacles in life. Maybe you can allow me to help you overcome your obstacles. The Bible says, 'Two are better than one, because they have a good return for their work; if one falls down, his friend can pick him up. But pity the man who falls and has no one to help him up!' Tray said, reciting the scripture his grandma Mabel had taught him and his little brother. "So I guess what I'm saying is, some things can't be overcome alone, and I want to be the help you need in order to overcome."

"Wow! Tray, you got a smooth answer for everything, don't you" she said with a huge smile on her face.

"To everything but to why you're so afraid to let me into your world. I'm not your enemy," he said.

"I know, but I barely know you. So I'll tell you what; we can be friends and see what that leads to, OK?" she asked.

"OK; but don't miss out on something good that could be what you need to have, all because you're afraid to let go of something that's already lost," he said. "Now let's enjoy some of this good ol' soul food."

As they ate and enjoyed more of one another's conversation, Desire couldn't take her eyes off of Tray. She kept thinking to herself; could anyone be this perfect, and could he be what her life needed?

Well, only time would eventually tell...

Chapter 13: The Good and the Bad

All week long Tray couldn't get Desire off his mind, and it wasn't long before Mona picked up on it.

"Tray, what's going on, babe?" she asked as Tray sat in a deep trance-like state. After not hearing her the first time, she repeated herself with more hostility: "Tray! I said, what's going on?"

As Tray snapped to attention, he immediately tried to act as if her aggravation concerned him.

"What's wrong, baby?" he asked her.

"You tell me. It's like you've lost all interest in me or something, nigga," she said with major attitude in her voice.

"Naw, lil mama. Never dat. I just had some shit on my mind lately, that's all."

"Nigga, that better be all. Don't let me find out you fuckin' on another ho, 'cause if I do, it's gonna get real ugly for you and the bitch. Straight up! Now, if you think I'm playin', test my gangsta," she said all up in his grill. Then, just like that, she smiled, kissed him on his cheek and said, "Now come on, we got a meeting."

Bipolar-ass bitch, Tray thought to himself. Actually, what he said was partially true. He had been having a lot on his mind lately. He couldn't help but compare the differences between the two women. One was his Bonnie and Clyde chick, ready to ride or die; the other was the kind to bring home to meet the family. One was sexy and gutter, the other was beautiful and classy. One threw herself into a relationship with him from the beginning, used to taking what she wanted, while the other was kind of shy, making Tray wait until she was able to give him her whole heart. She wasn't the type to half step, so was willing to wait until she was for sure the time was right for them both. The two girls were as different as night and day, because one was as deadly as taboo and the other as innocent as an unfulfilled fantasy. Tray was torn between the two.

When Tray came downstairs, the MOB $tars collective was already seated. Tray found a seat next to Mona, and then the meeting began.

"Welcome, $tars. Glad to see everyone could make it," Drak said with a smile on his face. He turned and looked at Tray as everyone, including Tray, enjoyed a quick laugh.

Drak continued: "Now, I called this meeting to let you know that we have some urgent business that must be handled. Most of you know Mack Maine. He isn't a MOB $tar member, but he invests money into our regiment in exchange for our protection and muscle. For those of you who aren't familiar with Mack Maine, he's a pimp from Vegas. He's been in our city for about three years. He initially got picked up on pandering charges and possession of a controlled substance. He said one of his hoes left some dope in his whip. Long story short; he kept it solid, did his time, then came out and jumped back on his hustle. So I kept my eye on him, and when the time was right, I introduced him to our operation. He declined membership, but was very interested in our ability to assure him that he, along with his stable of women, were guaranteed to be protected. He pays a monthly fee of $5,000, and anytime he's faced with a problem, he has our assistance -- as problem solvers.

62

"Now it seems that two of his top-of-the-line hoes were snatched up and brutally sodomized last week, and two days later, another was snatched up, made to smoke crack and then savagely raped. So, now the girls are scared to work, and he's calling on our assistance."

"So what's the plan, big bruh?" asked Lil Tech, the newest MOB $tar recruit, sharing his eagerness to fulfill his blood oath.

"Well, the first two girls were lucky and they were able to get a good look at two of the guys. They said one of the guys has a very distinct southern accent. They both say if they ever saw either of them again, they could identify them for sure. So we're gonna set up a trap for them that they will never forget; MOB!" Drak said.

"As one!" the crew said in unison then got up to leave.

Still thinking about Desire, he forced himself to stay more attentive to Mona while she was around. Walking up to her, he placed his arms on either side of her shoulder, gently kissed her and said, "I'm sorry if I made you feel I'd lost interest in you, baby. I love you, and don't you ever forget that, beautiful, you hear me?"

Wrapping her arms around his waist and placing her face next to his heart, she said, "I'm so in love with you, Tray, that you just don't understand to what length I'm willing to go in order to secure what's mine. And hopefully, I don't have to show you."

As she walked off, Tray couldn't help but catch the double meaning behind her words.

Later that day, Villian, Tray, and Lil Tech were in Yum Yum Donuts on Wilson Way when they heard a cat standing in line, talking on the phone in a very loud, deep southern accent.

"Ey, my nigga. That bitch talked all of that shit about having the best pussy in Northern Cali. Man, the bitch couldn't even take half of the dick. Now, her lil cousin was a champ. She had a dick in both hands, one in her mouth, all the while she's riding a dick. That bitch looked like she was auditioning for the next Stockton Gone Wild video. She 'posed to come through the spot tonight. Yeah, we still got rooms at the Econo Lodge next to California stop. We got room 229. Alright, come through, my nigga. One love," he said and hung up.

"Hey, sexy, how much for a dozen Maple Bars, a dozen Fritters and a dozen kisses from the woman of my dreams," the man with the southern accent said, causing the woman to smile as the crew gathered their order and left without a single word.

After reporting back with the information, a plan was put together, and by 9:00, it was ready to be executed.

It wasn't every day that the MOB $tars used outside influences to carry out missions, but made the exception with Trixie and Carmen because they were going to be the ones to positively identify the culprits.

Jungle and Bleek stayed in the room waiting for Brazy to slide through with the little bitch Macy. She was becoming infamous for her ability to take a dick all the way down the throat without gagging, and whose pussy was as tight as the Jaws of Life.

"Man, where is this nigga at, blood?" Bleak said to nobody in particular. "That nigga pro'ly on a side-street wit' dick all down the bitch throat 'bout to bring us some sloppy seconds."

"Nigga, I don't give a fuck about it being sloppy seconds. Hell, I'll go fifth! I jus' wanna be in line for some of that good shit. Straight up!" Jungle said as they both started laughing. "Nigga, fire up that blunt of Train Wreck."

Just as Bleek was lighting the blunt, there was a noise at the door. Quickly getting up and racing to the door, he saw the handle move. Looking out the peephole, he spotted a chocolate sister with dimples trying to open the door. Snatching it open, her and her friend jumped back.

"Ooohh! You scared us. How did you get in our room?" Mona asked, playing shocked.

"Baby, this is our room, but you're more than welcome to join us," Bleak said smiling.

"What? Oh, shit! This is 229, we're in 329. We are so sorry," she said.

"Don't be. Like I said, you're more than welcome, shawty."

"Naw, it's just me, wifey, and our strap on for now, baby. But if we change our minds, we'll call down here for you, sexy," she said, blowing him a kiss and palming Carmen's ass playfully as they started to leave. "What's your name?" she asked.

"Bleek," he said. "Just ask for Bleek."

"OK. I can definitely remember that; Bleak the Freak!" she said as they waved at him seductively and went through the doors.

Stepping back inside, Bleak said, "Nigga, you shoulda seen those freaky-ass broads. They said it's just them and their strap on. Shit! They better come fuck with this elephant trunk," he said as they both fell out laughing again. Suddenly Brazy and Macy walked through the door with their arms full of alcohol.

Let the fun begin, Bleek thought to himself.

As Mona and Carmen walked out the doors, Carmen spotted Brazy walking with a young thick girl who looked no older than 16, carrying arm-loads of alcohol with a smile on his face.

"There that other nigga go right there," she said.

"Are you sure?" Mona asked her.

"I couldn't be surer of anything in my life," Carmen said with hate in her eyes.

"OK, let's go," Mona said as she signaled the squad and gave Carmen a hug. "Bitch, don't even trip. We 'bout to handle this shit."

Chapter 14: Time for Some Action

As the trio took advantage of Macy's sexual skills, the phone started to ring. This caught them off guard since nobody other than them knew what room they were in. Besides that, when they wanted to communicate, they just called each other's cell phones.

Steady sliding in and out of Macy's asshole, Bleek reached over and picked up the receiver: "Hello?" he said into the phone.

"Is Bleek there?" the voice said softly.

"This is him. What's up?" he asked, not missing a stroke.

"Well, it sounds like you're already having fun," she said as she heard the moaning and grunting in the background. "We thought we would take you up on your offer, Bleak the Freek."

Realizing who was calling, he slid out of Macy's ass, wiped his dick off on her ass cheeks and said, "What's crackin', lil mama?"

"Well, we thought maybe you'd want to join us," she said in her naughty voice.

"Hell, yeah, I'll be right up."

"Oh, yeah; don't forget to bring you're A-1 game," she

66

said laughing before hanging up.

Oh, I never leave home without it he thought to himself as he washed up. He went to grab the burner, then decided he really didn't need it so he left it behind.

"Hey, y'all, I'ma be right upstairs," he said. But they were focused on Macy's sex game so they paid him no mind.

Taking the steps two at a time, he got to the door slightly out of breath. After knocking twice, the door was answered by a different broad than the ones from earlier. This one was Puerto Rican, half naked and smiling seductively.

"You must be Bleak the Freak," she said as she licked her lips and let her robe fall open, giving him a glimpse of her immaculate body.

"Every day of the week," he added to the quickly-catching-on phrase.

As Blaze let him in, Mona was laying across the bed, rolling a blunt, clad in nothing but a thong. Her legs were spread wide, giving him a view of her fat pussy lips and perfectly round ass.

"Hey, sexy, I'm glad you didn't let us down. Come on over here and have a seat," she said as she licked the blunt wrap.

As he sat on the bed beside her, he couldn't take his eyes off her ass. Looking up and catching him starting, she said, "See something you like?"

"Hell yeah," he said, smiling at her and rubbing his crotch.

Rolling onto her side and opening her legs, she thrust her finger into her pussy, placed them in his mouth and asked, "How you love the flavor?"

"Oh, I'm loving that" he said as he started to unzip his jeans.

She stopped him and said, "Hold on, Speedy Gonzalez. The pussy ain't goin' nowhere," as she patted his crotch.

Suddenly Blaze appeared, sat on his lap and said, "You

in for the longest fuck of yo' life, playboy," as she rocked back and forth on his lap.

"Now, here you go. Fire that up, sexy," Mona said, placing the blunt in his mouth and lighting it up for him. Taking a huge pull of the blunt smoke, he felt Mona start to unzip his pants and undo the bottom at the top before pulling his boxers and jeans off in one tug. As Bleak watched Blaze give him a slow strip tease, he suddenly saw the girl from earlier walk out of the bathroom with a robe tied around her petite frame, then quietly sit in a chair and watch. Believing he was in for a special treat, he focused 100% on Blaze's sensual self-foreplay. Not seeing the blunt when it was switched, Mona placed it to his lips as she put his hard penis in her mouth. Enjoying the warmness of her mouth, the visual stimulation from Blaze and the thought of being watched by an audience, he succumbed to the powerful state of lust as he inhaled deeply from the crack and PCP laced blunt. Before he knew it, his body was numb and his thoughts were racing, but he had no control of his bodily functions. He was able to see all that was happening, and was suddenly confused when the girl in the chair stood and untied her robe, revealing a huge strap-on penis. As he tried to ask her what it was for, his speech came out garbled. He felt like his tongue weighed a ton.

Seeing the look of confusion on his face, Carmen said, "What's wrong, baby, you don't think you can handle it?" repeating what he had said to her and Trixie the night of the incident. Reaching into her pocket, she came out with a jar of Vaseline and greased up the massive tool while she smiled at the look on his face. Grabbing and lifting his legs she said, "Shhhhhhh. This won't hurt a bit," as she slammed it to the hilt.

$$$$$

While Brazy was still trying to knock the lining out of Lacy's pussy, there was a knock on the door. "Dominoes

Pizza delivery," the voice said from the hallway.

Thinking that Bleek had probably ordered a pizza, he started to look for his boxers, but then thought to himself, since it was a female's voice, he'd give her a little peep show. When he opened the door, the lady in the Dominoes' Pizza uniform immediately looked down at his shriveled-up package, laughed and said, "Your pinky comes —I mean, your pizza comes to $14.95." She tried to stop laughing as she saw he was embarrassed.

Grabbing the pizza, he tried to cover himself. "I'll be right back," he said, cursing himself for allowing her laughter to get under her skin. Bitch! He thought to himself.

Now wearing his boxers, he came back to the door. As he opened it, he was face to face-to-face with a M-60 machine gun holding a 100-round drum on it.

"Turn around and get yo' bitch-ass back inside, nigga," Villian said as the crew rushed into the room. Once inside, Villian kicked Jungle in the ass and said, "What the fuck you doin' comin' to the door butt-ass naked like you John Holmes. Nigga, you ain't made like that. Nigga, there's more meat on that cheese pizza than what you workin' wit', shorty. Now sit yo' ass down 'fore I air yo' ass out." Turning the machine gun toward Brazy he said, "And what's up wit' you, nigga? You like takin' pussy, huh?"

"M-m-m-m-man, what you t-t-talkin' about?" he stammered nervously as he looked at all of them.

"M-m-m-man, what you talkin' about?" Villian mocked him. "Shut the fuck up! You know what the fuck I'm talkin' about!" He slammed the butt of the gun across Brazy's jaw. Blood splattered across Macy's breast as she shoved Brazy off her and curled up into a ball.

From behind the rest of the crew, Lil Tech walked out. "Word on the street is, playa, that you be takin' pussy, dog."

"Naw, I'm tellin' you, somebody's lyin', dog. You gotta believe me," he pleaded.

Suddenly Trixie snatched the Dominoes Pizza hat off and yelled, "Bitch, what the fuck you mean someone lyin'

69

on you!? Man yo' punk-ass up. You was all man when you sodomized me and my homegirl."

Snatching a banger from his waist, Tray stepped to Trixie and handed it to her. "Make this nigga own up to the error of his ways."

She accepted the cold blue steel, walked to the edge of the bed and stood in front of him; "What do you have to say, nigga, before I send you to hell?"

"I-I I'm sorry," he stammered. But before he could finish, she shoved the banger up under his chin and splattered brain matter all over the ceiling and wall.

In a flash, Lil Tech spun around and spit six Rhino slugs into the face and chest of Jungle. Drak snatched a screaming and crying Macy up by her throat and silenced her with a backhanded swipe across her larynx with a straight-edge razor. As they were leaving they heard a blood-curdling scream from the room above, then two shots fired in rapid succession followed by running feet.

The MOB $tars completed another successful mission and left behind a bloody scene of confusion and chaos. The night was left silent and there were no witnesses.

$$$$$

As Homicide Detective Brad Coleman entered the Econo Lodge parking lot, he was met by officer Niel.

"We have four bodies, sir. Three in room 229 and another in room 329. They don't seem to be related in any way, other than the victims being in various stages of undress," the officer said.

"Find the manager and see who each of the rooms were being rented to. I'm gonna do a walk-through and see what we're working with," Detective Coleman said as he walked toward the entrance.

As he walked down the hallway toward room 229, he couldn't help but notice the chill and the eerie feeling since entering the building. He spotted cigarette butts, crack baggies, a half-empty bottle of King Cobra, which could very possibly be urine; and, judging by the pissy smell that permeated the hallway, his money was on urine.

As soon as he entered room 229, he spotted a gentleman with several gunshot wounds to his upper chest with his head laid back on the windowsill. Congealed blood stuck to the window screen, ran down the wall and was puddled in his lap. Upon closer inspection, Detective Coleman could see that the victim had taken two bullets to the face. The first bullet had shattered the victim's cheekbone, and the second one had entered above the eye and blew
half the back of his head off.

The second victim actually looked like he was just an alcoholic sleeping off a good one. His body was bent over as he sat on the side of the bed with both of his arms hanging beside his legs. The only give-away was the huge hole in the top of his head and the puddle of blood surrounding his feet and dripping from the ceiling.

As he walked around the bed to get a better look at the female victim, he suddenly stopped cold. As he reached to move the hair out of the young girl's face, he whispered a silent prayer; "Please, God, just let it be a strong resemblance." Moving the blood-caked hair out of her face, he felt his stomach drop as his suspicion was confirmed. It was Macy, his niece.

The family had believed her to be away at Job Corps, getting a trade. What was she doing, holed-up in a motel room doing the unthinkable? She was only 16 for God's sake! Such a wasted life, he thought to himself. How hard it was going to be to break the news to his sister and the rest of the family.

The only noticeable wound that she had sustained was a lateral slice through the larynx, which was definitely enough to put an end to what was sure to be a long and promising life.

While he was still trying to clear his mind, he was

startled by officer Niel and the Medical Examiner, along with two Crime Scene Technicians.

"Detective Coleman, the M.E. and the Crime Scene Techs are here. I checked with the manager, and 229 was rented to an Edward Bailey, resident of Atlanta, Georgia. He's had the room for two weeks. 329 was rented to Lisa Bates, a resident of Sacramento. The room was rented for one day. Come on, let's let these guys get to work while I show you 329," the officer said as they left the room. When they reached the third floor, officer Niel said, "Now, this one is a little different."

"Different as in what?" Detective Colman asked curiously.

"Well... I'll let you see for yourself, sir," he said as they ducked under the crime scene tape and walked into the room.

Detective Coleman had seen a lot of murder scenes in 14 years of law enforcement, but nothing was as peculiar as what he walked into when he walked into room 329. Written in blood, on the wall in huge writing was: HERE LIES A SODOMITE!! The air was mixed with the scent of marijuana, lubricant and feces. A male victim was sprawled across the bed, face down with several cuts on his upper back. A massive black dildo was protruding from his anal cavity and he had suffered a bullet to the top of his spine and the back of his head. Just as he walked to the side of the bed, he stopped abruptly as he spotted what was unmistakably a severed penis. As he got a good look at the victim's face, he wasn't the least bit surprised at the look of horror that was plastered on it; it was a look that Detective Coleman would remember for as long as he lived.

Chapter Fifteen: Swagged Up

"Happy birthday, baby," Mona said as Tray rolled over, received a kiss and a small box that was wrapped and had a ribbon on top.

"Thank you, my love," he said as he accepted the gift.

"Go get ready. Everybody's waiting on you so they can give you your presents, OK?" she said enthusiastically.

"Alright, I'm gettin' up," he said as he sat up and tried to collect his thoughts. He'd had another nightmare, the third one of the week. All the killing was actually starting to have an effect on him.

After showering and dressing he opened his gift from Mona. Inside was a platinum and crushed-ice pinky ring in the shape of a king's crown. Inside the box was a tiny card that said, "To my king on his special day. Forever your gangstress, Mona." He couldn't help but smile because it was an excellent replica of what he'd showed her in a book, only his was ten times better!

When he came downstairs he was bombarded with happy birthdays, gifts, hugs, and birthday punches to his arms and legs, all done with love.

Suddenly Villain said, "We got another big surprise for you, bruh, but first..." He walked around Tray and placed a bandana over his eyes. As everyone guided him outside, he was suddenly stopped and told he can take the bandana off.

When Tray took the bandana off, he couldn't believe his eyes. It was the Cadillac CTS with a brand-new paint job —midnight blue, with a mural of Tray's face on the side! Under that it read: Get on my level! The custom plates read: 4U-2-NV. He felt like his heart was going to explode he was so full of joy. As Drak stepped out the Cadillac, he told Tray, "Test-drive this bitch!"

As Tray, Villian, Mona and Lil Tech jumped in to take it for a spin, Tray felt the seat automatically adjust to his comfortability. He felt like the luckiest nigga alive. Turning the music on, he was surprised to hear Mozzy's 'Bladadah' CD in the deck. Turning it up to volume 6, the speakers sounded like the inside of a concert as they listened to 'Body 4 Body' and cruised the hood.

$$$$$

Later that day, after drinking a little bit too much, Tray made the mistake of going to see his little brother to show off his new whip and to drop him off some new clothes. When he pulled up to the house, Damon was sitting on the porch looking bored out of his mind, but at the sight of Tray and his new whip he perked right up.

"Hey, Tray! Happy birthday, bro!" he yelled as he ran and gave Tray a hug. "Whose car is that? Its hecka clean," he said, not paying any attention to the mural of Tray's face on the side.

"It's mine, big-head," Tray said playfully, throwing a couple punches at his little brother who slapped his punches down and followed them up with a few of his own. "Alright, alright; you win lil Mike Tyson," Tray said, blowing his little brother's ego up.

Reaching into his pocket, he came out with a wad of bills and peeled his little brother off $400. "Don't let grandma see all this money, dog," he said.

"Tray, can I ask you something?" Damon asked him. "Anything, and anytime, bro," Tray said sincerely.

"Are you a drug dealer?" he asked curiously.

"Naw, why do you ask me that?" Tray said in return.

"Because, one day I was in your room playing your X BOX 360, and when I was looking for some games, I saw your necklace and it said MOB $tars. Plus, everybody says that the MOB $tars run the Central, and if you ain't hooked up with the MOB $tars and you try sellin' dope, then you could disappear. Is that true? 'Cause my friend Pedro be sellin' weed. I told him to stop, but..."

"Lil bro; no, I'm not a drug dealer. Yeah, I'm a MOB $tar, but it's not as bad as people make it sound. Your friend Pedro don't have no worries, OK? But don't mention that I'm a MOB $tar to grandma, alright?" Tray said after cutting his brother off. "Now come on, I got some clothes for you."

With his arms full of shopping bags, Damon rushed inside to try on his new clothes.

When Tray walked in, he saw his grandmother walking down the stairs. When she reached the bottom step she said, "Happy birthday, baby," and gave him a hug.

"Thank you, grandma," he said as he hugged her and gave her a kiss on the cheek. She immediately smelled the alcohol on him.

"Tray, didn't I hear you drive up and tell Damon that that's your car?" she asked him innocently.

"Yes, ma'am. Do you want to take a ride in it?" he asked.

"No, Tray. I wish you would be more responsible. If you're gonna drive, then at least you shouldn't drink alcohol," she said.

"I only had a little. I can handle it. And besides, I only came a few blocks."

"Tray, you sound foolish, it don't matter how far you comin' from. That's just an excuse that you're using to justify why you did what you did. I taught you to accept responsibility for your actions and to ask God for forgiveness, not to make excuses," she scolded him.

"Here we go with the God stuff! Where was God when --"

Cutting him off, she walked up on Tray, put her finger in his face and said, "As long as you're in my house and able to enjoy the very breath of life that you breathe, second after second, you will respect me. Don't you ever think you gon' come in *my* house and yell at *me*, lil boy. Don't you ever, and I mean *ever*, forget that, as for me and this household, we serve the Lord! If you can't control your demons, them maybe you need to move. I will not watch you destroy your life."

With tears welling up on her eyes, she tried to turn away so he wouldn't see her pain. Tray walked out the door, jumped in his car and pulled off without another word.

Later that day, after having consumed a fifth of Paul Masson, Tray sat in a stupor thinking of how his life felt like a pivot. On one side there were the things and people that were a representation of the good that life still promised him; but on the other side was all of the glitz, glamour and corrupt things that was sure to lead to prison or the graveyard. He knew what side he needed to choose, but the gravitational pull was much greater than his will and ability to escape the grips of death and destruction.

After having dozed off, he was awakened by a much too vivid nightmare. When he woke up he was both relieved and confused. As he kept trying to clear his thoughts, he kept seeing Bango one minute, then Desire the next. They were both taking turns cutting off his body parts while he begged and pleaded with them, but each time he asked for mercy, they would both say, "As you give, you shall receive!"

When he finally got his bearings together, he jumped on the phone and called Mona and the crew to come meet him, as he was still too drunk to drive.

The next morning he woke up with a raging headache. Hungover and dehydrated, he made it to the restroom after several failed attempts. He vowed to never drink like that again. After taking an ice-cold shower, he emerged from the restroom feeling like a new man and ready to face another day.

$$$$$

"Girl, you better quit playin'! I'll take 'im if you don't. Shiiit... that nigga is major swagged up. So, bitch, what is you gonna do; barbecue or mildew? You better get over Terrell. I understand that you loved him; but, girl, he's gone. Tray is alive. And fine as hell," said Spicy, trying to convince Desire to give Tray a chance.

"Dead or not, he's still Noah's father," she said softly, still a bit skeptical about Tray.

"Look, Dee; I understand that, but you deserve to be happy again. Now, you couldn't say Terrell wouldn't have wanted you happy."

"Yeah, I guess you're right," she said.

"So, you're gonna give him a chance?" Spicy asked enthusiastically.

"Yeah... I guess," she said with a smile on her face. "You better hope I don't get hurt," she added.

"Girl, you need to let him hurt that twat," Spicy teased.

"Bitch, shut up. You're so nasty; wit' yo' freaky ass," Desire said as she and Spicy laughed.

"Bitch, don't act like you ain't no freak, you just on hold right now. And I feel sorry for Tray when you unleash the beast!" she said as the two exploded in laughter again.

"Well, I'll call you later. I gotta run to the store. Love ya," Desire said.

"Love ya, too," Spicy responded before hanging up.

As Desire got ready for her daily runs, she thought of what Spicy said and enjoyed another laugh at her best-friend's boldness. Terrell, you may be gone, but you'll never be forgotten. Even if it kills me, I'm gonna find out who killed you, and they will pay in blood, Desire thought to herself.

Chapter 16: Mixed Emotions

As Tray was driving down California Street with the windows rolled up and the AC maxed out, he spotted a woman bent over with her G-string showing as she inspected the tire on her car. Figuring she probably needed help, he pulled up behind her and sat with his music vibrating the concrete as he watched her from behind, enjoying the view. Suddenly she stood up, turned toward him and smiled, showing off the beautiful gap between her two front teeth.

Stepping out of the car, Tray walked up to her, gave her a hug and a kiss on the neck. "Can I be of some assistance, gorgeous?" he asked suavely as he licked his lips and looked into her hazel eyes.

"Yeah, my tire has a slow leak. I'm scared to drive it like that. I might make it worse or even get into a wreck--"

Cutting her off with a kiss, he silenced her. "Get in my car," he said as he got into her car and drove it to Dubb City on Harding Way. While the workers put new rims and tires on her car, he took her to Hometown Buffet, her favorite restaurant. While they sat and talked, Tray just stared and admired her beauty.

"So, Tray, you done paid all of this money for this food

and you haven't even took a bite. What's up?" she said softly.

"Babygirl, that money ain't nothin'. The fact that you're here next to me and I'm able to enjoy your beauty and watch you be satisfied is worth every dime."

"Well, OK, Casanova; I'm 'bout to tear into this peach cobbler. And I'm warnin' you now, this might get ugly," she said as they both fell out laughing.

After watching her demolish two helpings of peach cobbler, they left a huge tip and departed. As they rode, Desire asked, "Tray, you're so sweat, charming, caring and compassionate. Why haven't some woman snatched you up yet?"

"Well, don't get it twisted; women try. But I don't want just any kind of woman. I want a woman who can truly appreciate the love that I have to offer rather than perceive it as weakness. I watched my mom endure mental, physical and emotional abuse, so I vowed that, when I find the right woman, I'm gonna treat her the way I wish those men would have treated my mom all those years, you feel me?" he said as he pulled into the parking lot of Dubb City.

"Yeah, I feel you," she said with a huge smile on her face, thinking to herself how he was too good to be true. When her car was brought out to her, she was thoroughly impressed because the 22-inch Diablo rims made her Cutlass look like a whole new car.

"Thank you," she said. "I truly appreciate everything. So, when can I see you again?" she asked shyly.

"Ooooh. So you want to see me again, huh?" he said teasingly.

"Yeah, something like that," she said as she playfully socked him in the arm.

"Well, I'ma have to check my -- naw, just kidding. We can get together this Friday night," he said with a smile on his face.

"OK, well, I guess... wait, today is Friday," she said.

"Well, I guess I'll see you tonight then, sexy," he said

kissing her lightly on the lips. "Wear something cute, I'll pick you up at 8."

"Alright, see you then," she said as she watched him drive off, thinking to herself how she hoped she wasn't making a mistake. She was feeling him -- in every way.

$$$$$

When Tray pulled up to the spot, he was greeted by Villian and Lil Tech who were sitting out front smoking a Kush blunt and sipping on a bottle of Remy Martin.

"What up, bruh?" said Lil Tech as he and Tray shook hands and embraced.

"Shit; ready to chief some of that Kush y'all blowin' on, dog," Tray said as Villian passed him the blunt and the two also embraced.

"Where you been, my nigga? You hard as hell to catch up to now that you're all whip-tastic," Villian said, teasing Tray as they started laughing.

Looking around before he spoke he said, "Man, I cracked this super-bad bitch, and she's feelin' your boy real tough. I need for y'all to cover for me tonight. I'ma tell Mona I gotta handle some business in the Bay. So if she asks one of y'all, back my play, fam."

"You already know; we got you, my nigga. But who's the bitch, and what her sister or mama hittin' fo'?" Lil Tech said as they all laughed.

"Y'all wouldn't know her; she's a good girl," Tray said, being evasive.

"Nigga, if you don't shut that shit up. Them be the freakiest! Look at yo' mama!" he said jokingly.

"Fuck you!" Tray said, still laughing. "At least I had a mama. You was born in High Desert, ya booty baby," he shot back as they all busted up laughing. "And you came out the booty wit' a beard and buck teeth, bitch!" he continued.

After they were finished playing the dozens, Tray gave

81

them some dap and went upstairs to put his plan in motion. When he walked into the room, Roxy, Blaze, and Mona were in the room being loud and obnoxious as they had their own little get-together. Once they saw him in the room, their laughing quieted to naughty giggles.

"Hey, babe," Mona said. "Do you need the room?" she asked.

"Naw, I'm just changing. I have to run out to Frisco tonight," he said.

"Well, you might wanna wear a coat 'cause it gets chilly at night down there, babe," she said as she got up and walked into the walk-in closet behind him, gave him a blunt, dropped to her knees, pulled his boxers down and swallowed his tool all the while stroking him aggressively. When he was fully erect, she pushed him back up against the wall of the closet, turned around, slid onto him, braced herself against the opposite wall and started to slam herself onto his pole with so much force it was like she was trying to punish herself. Suddenly what had started as a low moan was turning into an audible plea, and then full outright cries of both pleasure mixed with pain as she milked him dry. Still trying to catch his breath, he was wondering what that was all about. She hadn't gotten that freaky in a minute. Not that he was mad at her, of course, just shocked and exhausted.

As he walked out of the closet and headed toward the restroom, all eyes were on him, and right before he closed the door he heard Mona say, "Now, take that to the Bay with you. Let that bitch know I said what's up, and have fun enjoying my sloppy seconds. I told you, nigga, that's my dick, and don't you forget it. Now have fun. Real boss bitch on deck! Signin' off!"

As he was in the shower, he couldn't help but think of the pain she was covering up in front of them. What she's expressing as aggression was really her defense mechanism to protect her from exposing her bruised ego. He was going to have to make a choice between the two girls soon and he

82

was not looking forward to that day. He loved the one and was infatuated with the other. What had he gotten himself into; and, better yet, how would he get himself out of it?

Dressed and ready to go but not wanting to seem too eager, he sat down next to Mona, kissed her on the neck and massaged her gently; she tried to ignore him by acting like she was too interested in girl-talk to be distracted by his advances. When he saw that she was going to keep ignoring him, he stuck his tongue in her ear. That always get her attention.

Suddenly she turned to him and said, "Don't be rude and leave the bitch waiting, Tray. I'll be here, I ain't goin' nowhere. But when she hurts you, don't say I didn't warn you, nigga. I'm all you need, but since you ain't happy with what you got, go on and chase after what it is you think you want."

She kissed him lightly on the bottom lip, then turned back and continued listening to the girl-talk as he got up to leave quietly.

Chapter Seventeen: A Night to Remember

As Tray stopped at the liquor store, he got a fifth of Hennessey, a case of Red Bull energy drinks, and stopped out south to pick up an ounce of White Widow and 3 Blue Dolphin X pills before heading to Desire's.

After knocking on the door, Noah peeked out the window, smiled at him then opened the door. "It's Tray!" he shouted happily as he grabbed ahold of Tray's hand, pulled him inside and gave his leg a tight hug. "I missed you, Tray," he said.

"I missed you, too, lil man. Here you go," he said as he handed Noah a bag.

Eager to see what it was, he sat the bag down, reached inside and yelled loudly, "Oh, my God, mama, it's an XBOX 360! Yay!" He ran past his mom in search of Ms. Daisy.

"Keep on, you won't be able to get rid of him. He's already been buggin' me every ten minutes; 'When is Tray coming? Where is Tray at? When Tray comes, tell me, mama. Did Tray come yet'? Desire said as Tray laughed so hard his stomach was cramping. "It ain't funny, Tray, he's driving me crazy all 'cause of you bein' so nice to him."

"That's alright, baby. You'll be alright. Are you almost ready?" he asked, still smiling at her.

"Boy, I been ready. Give me one minute," she said and walked off, only to return shortly with a look of frustration on her face as she flopped down on the couch. "Will you hook that game up for him before I lose my mind, Tray?"

Laughing at her as she sat seething, he walked over to where she was, bent down and kissed her tenderly. Just like that, she was smiling again. "Give me five minutes," he said before strolling off as cool as a cucumber.

After leaving the house, Tray opened Desire's door and whispered in her ear, "I forgot to tell you, but I think you should know you are definitely a dime-piece. I don't know if I want to dance the night away with you, or dip you in chocolate and devour you right here, lil mama," he said as she blushed as red as her wrap-around Chanel dress that fit like a glove and left little to the imagination.

Before getting into the car he popped the trunk, retrieved a bag and placed it on her lap. When she opened it, she spotted three jewelry boxes. Inside the first was a ladies Movado watch, inside the second was a platinum promise ring, and the third box contained a 24 karat rose gold figaro link necklace that held a solid gold medallion with Ecclesiastes 4:9-12 inscribed on the face: 'Two are better than one...'

"Tray, these are so beautiful. But, they are also too expensive," she said softly.

"Desire, you're beautiful and you deserve beautiful things. These are only small tokens of my appreciation for you allowing me to be a part of you and Noah's lives. So quit worrying about the value of these material things, and let's start focusing on the value in one another. Now, let's go enjoy ourselves," Tray said as he started the car and the melodic sounds of Ronald Isley filled the car.

As soon as he jumped on the highway he told her, "Fire up that blunt in the ashtray."

Although it wasn't Desire's normal practice to smoke

weed, she did as he asked without complaining. There was something about Tray that allowed her to overlook any of her inhibitions and just relax and go with the flow. And go with the flow is exactly what she did.

She leaned back in her seat and drifted off on a cloud of euphoria from a mixture of the White Widow combined by the intoxicating effects that Ronald Isley's voice was having on her as he sung a ballad about riding on a highway that leads to love. She couldn't help but think of how similar tonight felt to the exact words that Ronald Isley was singing. Could tonight actually lead to love? She wondered as she looked over at Tray, who was such an enticing mystery. Smiling to herself, she watched the reflections from the passing lights glint off of his expensive stunna shades as he bobbed his head to the music, oblivious to her observing him.

Suddenly she was disturbed by a thought; she found herself comparing him to Terrell. Where Terrell was thuggish and rough, Tray was gentle and charming. Where Terrell had difficulty expressing his love to her at times, Tray had no difficulty being affectionate, was never at a loss for words or lacking the ability to make her feel special. They were as different as night and day. She was struggling to try and separate her feelings for the two. One was gone, but whom she still loved deeply, and the other she was infatuated with. She was truly starting to believe that Tray was the missing piece to the incomplete puzzle her life had become.

When they pulled up into the parking lot of Club Mirage, they reached into the back seat, grabbed the bag containing the Hennessey and Red Bull, then made them both a cup. By the time they entered the club they were completely feeling themselves.

As they found seats and were getting situated, the club suddenly rocked with Rick Ross' song "God Forgives and I Don't." The two began showing off their moves as they let the music captivate them. In no time they were both as sweaty as a death row inmate on his way to the electric chair. Unbeknownst to Desire, she was feeling the effects of the Blue Dolphin that Tray had let dissolve in her drink while in the car.

"You ready to breeze, lil mama?" Tray asked when he saw her nipples were as hard as Jawbreakers.

"Yeah, let me go to the restroom first, though," she said as she walked off. When she got to the stall she was all smiles. She was really enjoying Tray's company. Turning around and reaching under her dress to pull her panties down, she fell out laughing as she realized she had been so excited and in a rush to be ready for Tray to pick her up that she'd ran off and left her panties on the bed.

A lady in the adjourning stall heard her and called over, "Are you alright over there?" she asked. Catching her breath long enough to explain it to her, they both started to laugh.

"Damn, bitch! He must be some kind of special muthafucka. Shit, I wish I could meet a muthafucka special enough to make me forget my panties," she said as they continued to laugh.

"He's gonna think I'm some kind of freak," Desire said, trying to compose herself.

"Then if I was you, I wouldn't disappoint him," she said as they fell out laughing again.

After introducing themselves to one another, exchanging numbers and promising to stay in touch, the two went their separate ways.

With a giant smile plastered on her face, she walked up to Tray, kissed him fully on the lips and said, "I'm ready," with a naughty look in her eyes.

With a giant smile on his face as well, he whispered, "I'm right behind you, baby."

As Desire picked up on the double meaning his comment held, she blushed a crimson shade and sashayed off seductively.

Once they were in the car, Tray looked over at Desire

and contemplated the idea of asking her if she felt comfortable going to the motel for the rest of the night, when suddenly Desire looked over at him and said, "So, is that all you had planned for the night?" as she poured him another cup of Hennessey and Red Bull concoction.

"Well, I don't know what all you're able to handle, lil mama," he said, trying to test her to see if she had certain limits.

"OK, smartass! I'm gonna put it like this; I ain't scared of the dick, so what it hit fo'?" she said while seductively looking at him over the rim of the cup as she took a sip.

With a look of cockiness he said, "Don't let your mouth write a check that yo' pussy can't cash." He laughed at his creative words.

"Whatever comes out of my mouth, best believe my pussy can back it up," she shot back in return as she took another sip of the drank.

Starting to feel a little intimidated, he had to reach over and take a huge gulp from his cup as he turned up the sounds and searched for the nearest Howard Johnson hotel.

When they entered the room, Tray immediately started surfing the channels in search for the porn station. After learning there wasn't one, Desire came out of the restroom and said, "Nigga, what I'm 'bout to put on yo' ass, you ain't gon' be interested in no porn no way. So you can turn that shit off and strip," as she fired up the rest of the blunt.

Chapter 18: The Climax

While Mona sat alone smoking a blunt and watching the remastered version of Scarface, her thoughts kept drifting and picturing Tray fucking another bitch. No matter how hard she tried to focus on the movie, her thoughts seemed to keep drifting. So she got up, turned off the TV and left the room. Sitting in the entertainment room proved to be monotonous as Blaze and Roxy talked and joked about the same ol' shit. So, after only a couple minutes, she decided to go out south to buy some X pills and some more Kush. Philthy and G-Rock, whom Drak and his MOB $tars had run out of Stockton for selling weight on MOB turf had never actually left Stockton, they just let Deuce sell their weight for them. Over the months they had done some investigating and had come to learn that the raid they had been hit with was actually a robbery set up by Drak, the leader of the MOB $tars -- a dirty cop. They had vowed to get revenge when the time was right, because dirty or not, cop killing would get you the death penalty, or at the very least, life without parole. Until the time came, they kept their business inconspicuous.

$$$$$

As they matched each other stroke for stroke while looking into each other's eyes, Desire rode Tray with a pent-up passion that could only be described as begging to be released. Grinding back and forth and biting her bottom lip, she was suddenly overcome by a pleasure so intense that her eyes rolled deep into her head, and her whole body became so rigid that she seemed to be possessed by some kind of demon as she started to buck wildly.

"Ooooohh... Oohhhh shit, baby... Oohhh, baby, I'm 'bout to cum. Here it cum. Here it cum. Here. It. Cuuummm!" she yelled as she released and squirted her juices all over his stomach and thighs. Then, before he could urge her on, she turned around reverse cowgirl style and got back to getting it!

$$$$$

As Philthy and G-Rock sat in the Avalanche with the Louis Vitton paint job, sitting on 27-inch rims, Philthy was rolling a blunt of Kush that he had just purchased from Mando, the Kush and pill man, when suddenly G-Rock spotted a familiar face.

"Hey, Philthy, ain't that the lil bitch that was wit' them MOB $tar cats the day they pulled that fake-ass raid on us and got us for them bricks and that dough?"

"Hell, yeah, that's her sexy ass. What you thinkin', my nigga?" Philthy asked as he sparked a flame to the blunt.

"I say we rock this bitch to sleep, dog."

"It is what it is, my nigga. Let's wait for this bitch off in the cut like Neosporin, and when the time is right we'll give this bitch the bidness," he said as he laid his seat back, took a big pull off the Kush blunt and waited.

$$$$$

"Damn, Mona; when are you gonna quit playin' and give a nigga some ass, girl?" Mando asked trying to sound sexy.

"Damn, Mando; when you gon' let a bitch stick her finger in *yo'* ass, nigga?" she mocked him jokingly. "You gave bubba some in prison, why I can't hit that shit?" she continued as she playfully pinched him on his ass while his boys started laughing at him.

"Yeah, I want some, too, dog," his partner said playfully and tried to pinch the other cheek. Swatting his hand away, the two started to shadow box as Mona was handed the Tequila bottle.

Actually, Mona would have been giving Mando some pussy, but there were too many rumors that his dick was dirty with STDs.

After kicking it with them for a while, Mona purchased her goods and left. She had a craving for some In-N-Out Burger that was starting to get the best of her; her stomach growled and it felt like it was trying to eat its way to her uterus. As she jumped in the car and started it, she noticed a dark brown Avalanche on big rims sitting up the block and could've sworn the passenger was watching her through the side-view mirror, but figured it was probably a nigga jockin' her style like always. As she drove past them she looked in their direction but they were looking down at something it seemed. So, going on about her business, she turned down Airport Way, but once she spotted the Avalanche following her, she reached into her purse, slid the 14-shot 9mm onto her lap and continued to watch her rear-view.

$$$$$

"Oh, baby!" Desire said again as she was swept up into another wave of pleasure. "I think I'm... I think... I think I'm about to... cum, daddy.... Oh, shit; oh, shit; oh, shit... Here it comes, baby... Ahhh!" she yelled as she clawed at his legs while cumming for the fifth time.

$$$$$

"I say we knock this bitch down at the light," G-Rock said as Philthy jacked a round into the chamber of the Desert Eagle. When he saw her stopped at the light, he was rolling his window down when he realized he'd fucked up in a major way and was staring death in the face.

Anticipating their ambush, she waited patiently as she watched them roll up on her. Determined to go out like a boss bitch, she opened the door and jumped out, busting as she walked toward them. The last thing she saw was the look of anguish on the passenger's face as the Rhino slugs chewed through the engine, dashboard, and finally his flesh before the Avalanche knocked her ten feet into the air. She landed two feet from her idling car as the Avalanche turned onto Charter way and escaped into the night.

$$$$$

Tray and Desire laid in a puddle of sweat- and semen-soaked sheets, thoroughly exhausted from their sex marathon. Neither could speak for several minutes as they laid there dehydrated.

"Wow! That was the bidness" she said as she looked over at Tray, who could only nod in agreement. "I needed that," she added as she wiped her sweat-soaked hair out of her eyes and face, continuing to fan herself even though the AC was on.

Tray laid there still in a daze, trying to pull himself from the sexual bliss. He had never been so thoroughly sexed in his entire life. He couldn't help but acknowledge the unbelievable gravitational pull he had experienced during his earth-shattering climax. It felt like he was being pulled in different directions by some kind of unseen force, but as he laid there spent, he had to say that he was definitely addicted to the lust that both of his women unleashed on him, and he was going to have one hell-of-a time separating from or choosing between the two.

After returning from the restroom on unsteady legs, Desire wiped Tray down from his head to his feet, returned the soapy rag to the bathroom, then towel-dried him off.

Having completed her ritual, she laid next to him and placed her head on his chest above his heart, played with the hairs on his stomach and softly said, "Tray, don't hurt me and Noah. We've been through enough already. We are still trying to get over the death of his father."

"Oh, yeah, you never got to tell me about that. I just wanted you to tell me about it in your own time. I know how losses can be, and how they can have an effect on families; especially children that are small," Tray said understandably. "If you don't mind me askin', what happened?" he asked curiously.

After hesitating, finally she said, "He... he was murdered. Earlier this year. He had just left me and Noah. We had just come from borrowing a few dollars so he could buy Noah some Pampers, but he never made it back. They found him beaten and shot in the back of the head, still clutching the few bloody dollar bills in his balled-up fist. I asked around and begged to know what had happened to him. Nobody would tell me until it finally came out that those bitch-ass MOB $tars are the ones who did it and destroyed me and Noah's lives.

"Who was your baby's father?" he asked, but already knew the answer.

"His name was Terrell Hopkins, but his hood name was Bango. And it just tears me up every time I see Noah's face 'cause he looks identical to his father. When I see how Noah is with you, it is such a relief. I was so scared that his life would suffer because of our loss, but it's almost as if God heard all of my deepest heart-felt prayers and sent me you, my very own angel," she said as Tray felt the wariness and the slight tingle as her tears touched his chest, then rolled down his ribcage.

Focusing on keeping his breathing steady, he couldn't help but think of how such a beautiful night could end in so much pain.

As the sound of her light snoring reached his ears, Tray found himself praying to God for forgiveness for murdering Terrell, as well as other sins that had been eating him alive. He didn't sleep a wink as Desire slept like a baby.

Chapter 19: No More Pain... Please!

As Tray and Desire rode back to Stockton, she noticed Tray was unusually quiet and wouldn't look her in the eyes, so she decided to break the silence.

"So, are you usually this quiet after getting your world rocked, lil daddy?" she asked with a huge smile on her face as she reached over and rubbed his package seductively.

As he forced a smile, he looked over at her and said, "I wouldn't know. That was the first time I had my world rocked," as they both started laughing.

Reaching into the center console, Tray passed her another blunt and told her to fire it up. As the two enjoyed their first blunt of the day, Desire told Tray about leaving her panties as she rushed to be prepared for him. This caused another round of laughter, but shortly after they were each in their own zones again. Desire was caught up in the rapture as she let the smooth voice of The Weeknd envelope her, while Tray continued to think of the fact that he was the cause of Desire and Noah's pain.

As they pulled up to her house, he had to reach over to wake her up. Realizing she was home, she yawned, looked over at Tray and said, "Are you gonna come in for a while?"

"Naw, I need to get home. I'll call you later, lil mama. Give Noah a hug for me, OK?" he said.

"OK. Well, thank you for the beautiful evening, Tray, and the beautiful gifts," she said as she reached over and kissed him, then got out of the car and headed inside.

Deciding to shoot out south to snatch up a few X pills since he knew he was going to have some making up to do, he headed toward Charter Way. As he was approaching Airport Way, he noticed that the traffic was congested. When he was debating if he should just look for a way to get out of the traffic jam, he spotted Mona's car surrounded by an ambulance, fire engines and police cars. The Scene was yellow-taped off and the police were trying to keep the spectators at a distance. Suddenly Tray spotted Drak, Villian and Blaze; Blaze was crying on Villian's shoulder. As Tray's stomach dropped, he tried not to jump to conclusions. Maybe it was just an accident, he thought to himself.

Pulling to the curb and parking, he jumped out and made his way through the crowd. When he finally reached Villian and Blaze, she turned around and ran into Tray's arms.

"The bastards killed her!" she said as she broke down in a fit of sobbing pain. She balled her fists up in his shirt as sobs continued to wrack her body.

As Tray stood stunned, he looked at Villian and asked, "What the fuck happened, dog?"

"Man, we still tryna find out. Drak has more info on what's goin' on. He went in to work, and as soon as he heard about this shit, he called us," Villian said, wanting to console Tray but not really sure how.

As a look of pain washed over his face, the realization of the fact that, while he was away with Desire fulfilling the desires of his lust for her, Mona was alone, facing whatever was the cause of her demise. When she was in a situation where she needed him the most, he was nowhere to be found. That would always be one of the most hurtful, self-inflicted scars to his heart.

"Man, I got to find out what happened to her. Somebody gots to pay, dog," Tray said with both of his fists balled up. "Nigga, you know the rule: eye for an eye! Since somebody took what was mine, and ours, then it's our duty to make sure they feel the burn from the flame that they've ignited," he added as tears of rage filled his eyes.

After the medical examiner came and picked up the body, the crowd of spectators started to thin out as they became bored with the whole incident. Tray, Villian and Blaze left as well, heading back to the spot to wait and hear what kind of information Drak had found out.

As they pulled up the the house, several members of the MOB $tars were standing around, talking. When they saw Tray and them, they all came and embraced him, gave him their condolences and promised to help find out what had happened to Mona.

After getting away from the crew, Tray just wanted to be alone to internalize all that he had come up against in just a matter of hours. It was like his whole world was starting to crumble all around him. Closing his eyes and shutting out the world, he soon dozed off into a deep and much-needed sleep...

"Man, I only got a few dollars to buy my lil son some Pampers."

"Tear it off!..."

"I'm sorry, I panicked..."

"Mark-ass nigga! Empty yo' pockets, bitch nigga!" BOOM! BOOM!...

"I'm sorry, I panicked..." BOOM! BOOM!...

Tray snatched himself from the nightmare, feeling Bango's spirit tormenting him. As sweat poured from his body, he rushed into the restroom, rinsed his face and looked into the mirror as bloodshot eyes stared back. Suddenly he got down on one knee and started to pray.

"God, please hear me as I humbly come before you,

asking for your help. I've lost my way. I went after the lusts of my flesh. I took something that was perfect and precious to you, father, a life, and I stand before you asking for your forgiveness and mercy. I ask for your strength to do what I know I need to do to make amends."

Then Tray raced out the house, jumped into his whip and smashed off as the crew watched with concern.

Pulling up to Ms. Daisy's house, he parked, knocked on the door and waited. Suddenly the door was opened and Desire happily invited him inside.

"Oh; my; God. This boy soooo loves this game, or so he keeps saying!" she said, mocking Noah as she laughed.

When Tray barely smiled, she stopped and started to get worried. "Baby, what's wrong?" she asked curiously, then threw her arms around him to comfort him when she spotted tears in his eyes.

"Come on, let's go upstairs," she said. But he shook his head and didn't budge.

"Naw, I better not," Tray said while looking down. "I think we should talk here."

"Talk! Tray, what the fuck is going on!? Don't do this shit to me and my baby. Please! No more pain, please!" she said as tears flooded her hazel eyes.

"I didn't know, baby. I did not know," he said repeatedly with a voice full of pain.

"Know what, Tray?" she snapped, thoroughly confused. "Tell me!"

"I'm a MOB $tar!" he snapped back at her. "There. Are you happy? I'm a MOB $tar."

Standing with both hands over her face and sobbing; "God, no, don't let this be happening to me, God. This is too much to handle, too soon, Father," she prayed softly as she steadily sobbed, pleaded with God and shook her head repeatedly.

"There's more," Tray said, but was immediately cut off before he could continue.

"Oooohhhh, God... Nooo, nooo, nooo!" she wailed.

"I was there when Bango was killed," he said, softer than he intended to.

Taking her hands from her face she asked, "Why are you saying these things to me, Tray? Why do you want to hurt me? What did I do to fuck up? Tell me!" she pleaded with him.

"Why are you crying, mama?" Noah asked her.

Hurrying to wipe her eyes and compose herself, she said, "I'm not, baby," she said with a shaky voice. Then she faked a smile and turned to comfort her son. "Tray was playing a wolf in sheep's clothing to us. I'm sorry I put you through all of this, Noah. Now, tell the big bad wolf bye-bye," she coaxed him.

"Mommy, what's the wolf in sheep's clothing?" he asked inquisitively.

"Somebody who acted like he wanted to be a part of our family, but now that he got what he wanted, he doesn't need the sheep suit anymore," she said accusingly, trying to plant a hate-for-Tray-seed in his young mind.

"Can I have a sheep suit?" Noah asked innocently. But Desire ignored him.

"Before you go; who did it?" she asked with hate in her eyes, hurt in her voice and pain written all over her face.

Without saying a word, Tray's silence spoke louder than he could have ever spoken. As he turned and walked back out the door, leaving Desire devastated, she collapsed, sobbing on the floor.

After driving around for hours deep in thought and pain, he told himself there was one more thing he needed to do.

When he pulled up, before he could even get out of the car he was overcome with a great sense of peace, and suddenly he realized everything would be all right.

As he knocked at the door, it was suddenly rammed into him as Grandma Mabel burst out the door and wrapped her arms around Tray. As tears of joy filled her eyes, she squeezed him tight. "Dear God, thank you for answering my prayers. He was lost, but now he's found. Praise the Lord!" she shouted and praised. "I love you, baby," she said to Tray.

"Grandma Mabel, I love you, too, and I'm sorry for disrespecting you, our house, my lil brother, and most importantly, God. Please forgive me. I'm begging you," he pleaded with her.

"Baby, I've been forgave you. Come on in here!"

"Tray!" Damon exclaimed happily when he saw his brother. Running and embracing him he asked, "Are you moving back home?"

As Tray looked over his shoulder at Grandma Mabel, she nodded her head hopingly.

"Yeah, I'm home, bro," he said as he started to trade blows with him playfully,

Grandma Mabel just watched, smiled, and silently praised God as she thought to herself, my very own prodigal son.

"I hope you know you ain't gettin' your room back," Damon said playfully, rushing to show Tray the changes and upgrades that he had made to his old room.

Chapter 20: Gettin' out the Game

It had been two weeks since the beauty of Tray's two worlds had suddenly collided. He was doing his best to stave off his desires to avenge Mona's death, all the while fighting off the demons that were still attacking him due to his participations in the loss of other lives — mainly Bango's.

Suddenly coming to the conclusion that he had to sever his ties with the MOB $tars, he grabbed a backpack, filled it with various MOB paraphernihia, said a prayer asking for protection and guidance, then left the house. He was on a mission to put an end to what should've never been.

When he pulled up to the spot, he was shocked to see that there were only a few MOB $tars around. Villian, Mack, Roxy, and Lil Tech all greeted and embraced him, which he accepted greatfully.

"Tray 8, we found out that those mark-ass niggas Philthy and G-Rock, the Bay Area cats that were selling weight on our turf and we had to run off awhile back, they were the ones behind Mona's death. But the word on the street is that she took that nigga Philthy out before G-Rock got her, if that makes you feel any better," Villian said hopefully.

Shaking his head, Tray said softly, "Naw, that don't make me feel no better, bruh." Looking around at all of their faces he added, "Ain't y'all tired of all this death and destruction? Man, this ain't the way life is supposed to be. Mona was my heart. I knew the hurts and hangups she struggled with, and just like that, she's gone!"

"Look, bruh, we understand your pain and loss, and don't think for a minute that we don't feel the pain; we knew her longer than you. But, life has to go on; forward motion!" Villian said, trying to convince Tray. "That's how the game is played, lil bruh. They take one of ours, we take five of theirs; it's nothin'! Now, you're either a lion or a lamb, and the power you acquire will be a direct reflection of which one you are. And, Tray, we lions, bruh!"

"Don't you know that you can have all the power in the world, the riches and the glory, and still not be victorious? God has chosen the weak things in the world to put to shame the things which the world may perceive to be mighty?" Tray said, rebuking Villian.

"So what is you sayin', Tray? That you're gonna let Mona get murdered, and now you don't want retribution to fall on the nigga's head that's responsible because, all of a sudden, you on some holy ghost shit, blood!?" Lil Tech snapped at Tray. With a severe mean mug on his face, he repeatedly pounded his open palm with his fist in an aggressive attempt to emphasize his feelings of betrayal on Tray's part. "Nigga, and I'm 'post to be yo' off-breed? Fuck you!" he added before walking into the house and slamming the door.

"Tray, don't sweat that, bruh. That lil nigga just got a lot of anger and hurt built up in him, plus he's a hot head. But, seriously, Tray, what's up?" Villian asked his protégé.

"Tyson, man, you know this shit ain't cool, what we're doin'. Man, I'm tired of seeing dead bodies, causin' pain to peoples' lives and breaking up families," he said, calling Villian by his government name to put emphasis on how serious he was.

"So, basically, you're tryna walk away from our family? The family that paved the way to your success? We made you who you are today, Tray," he said.

"That's the thing, bro; I don't even like what I've become, dog, because it's not me. And I've decided to finally live out my own identity, and, win, lose or draw, I'm out!" Tray said as he took the backpack off his shoulder, sat it down and turned to walk away. Suddenly he stopped, reached into his waist, pulled out the banger, then came back and sat it next to the backpack.

Mack and Roxy were the first to approach him; "No matter what, Tray, we will always love you, lil homie. If you ever need anything, we're here, baby boy," Mack said as he and Roxy embraced him. Suddenly Mack popped the trunk of his new Rolls Royce Phantom, reached inside and pulled out a diamond encrusted Rolex watch with a hologram of Tray's and Mona's picture on the face. The inscription on the back said: Forever, as one!

"She wanted to get out as well, and she wanted to marry you, Tray. That's what we were talking about that night you came in the room and announced you had to run to Frisco. She already had the money paid on all the arrangements. She was just gonna let it be a surprise wedding. She wanted it to be on August 29th, because that was the day her mom passed away and she's deemed it the worst day of her life. But, by marrying you on that day, it would have changed to the best day of the rest of her life; your anniversary, and the closing of a door on a past she no longer wanted to remember," Roxy said with tears in her eyes.

Suddenly Villian came over and gave him a hug. "You know where I'm at, my boy. Don't be no stranger. And, oh, yeah, say a prayer for me, bruh," said Villian with a look of admiration on his face as he released his grip on their embrace.

"You know I got you, bro. You know, you're always invited to come to our church; it ain't like you don't know where it is," Tray said with a smile on his face as he saw that Villian was going to stand behind the image he had built for himself.

"Whoa, whoa, whoa, lil TD Jakes, I'm on my own mission right now. And besides, I need to get myself right," Villian said.

"Homie, you don't go to God when you get yourself right. You go to God so he can help you get yourself right," Tray corrected him. "But, whenever you're ready, just know that He always has open arms and He's waiting for you to accept his loving embrace," he added as he said his farewells and left with a feeling of elation.

Later that evening, he decided to go to church with his grandma Mabel for Bible study. He knew that the only way for him to release some of the negative thoughts and feelings inside him was to find ways to replace them with more positive and constructive ones.

When they arrived, they were greeted by pastor Saffold. "Hello, Mabel, Tray and Damon. We're glad you are able to come and join us. We were just about to go to Saint Joseph's Hospital. Ms. Daisy suffered a stroke. They say it was massive and they don't know if she's gonna pull through. So we all thought we'd at least go out there and pray over her and offer our support," he said enthusiastically.

"Well, I'm all for it, pastor. Any way I can be of assistance, count me in," Grandma Mabel said.

Tray couldn't help but wonder if this had happened as a result of his role in the murder of her grandson. Had Desire told her what she'd learned?

When they arrived at the hospital they were met by several members of their church. Tray didn't see Desire and Noah so he decided to go grab a few things from the gift shop. After purchasing his few items, he went back to the group of other church members who were on their way to Ms. Daisy's room.

When they arrived, they were allowed in the room for a short period of time. As Tray entered the room, the first thing he noticed was a puffy-eyed, slightly disheveled but still beautiful Desire, sitting beside the bed with Noah on her lap. At the sight of Tray, he jumped off her lap, dashed through the church members' legs with an agility that would have impressed any NFL scout, all the while saying "There go Tray, mama. Mama, there go Tray. Tray, I missed you soooo much," he said as he wrapped his arms around Tray's waist and squeezed tightly.

After handing his gifts to a lady standing nearby smiling, he picked up Noah and hugged him affectionately. When he looked at Desire, she had a look of thankfulness on her face. As he walked over to her with Noah still in his arms, he put his other arm around her and whispered in her ear, "I'm sorry." She wrapped her arms around his waist and tears filled her eyes as she gently placed her head on his chest.

As the room was filled with intercessory prayers for Ms. Daisy, Desire was saying an intercessory prayer for Tray. She told herself that, if he asked for forgiveness, she'd forgive him. She felt that, as long as he was able to repent and make an attempt to live a better life, then she could accept his past, but she would have to see what he was willing to sacrifice; the life of a thug or the life of a family man. But he would have to choose because she couldn't allow Noah to keep being hurt; he loved Tray too much. And she could see what Tray felt for him was genuine. She was even willing to take Tray to Bango's gravesite and allow him the opportunity to make amends to Bango in the spirit.

As everyone was leaving the room, Tray looked in her eyes and asked, "So, does this mean that you can forgive me? 'Cause I'm so sorry I was the cause of your heartache."

"Baby, of course I forgive you. But what's more important is that you repent and ask God to forgive you."

"I already did," he said, cutting her off. "And I divorced the MOB $tars today, too."

"Really, Tray?" she exclaimed. Then the thought hit

her: "But, can you do that? They won't try to kill you or anything, will they?" she asked with a worried look on her face.

"Naw, I don't think so. Everything seemed alright when I left. But, regardless, I'd rather die for doing what's right than to die because I'm living wrong, feel me?" he said as he gave her his signature lip lick and smile, causing her to blush, like always.

"Tray, I love you so much. You make Noah and I unbelievably happy, and nothing in the past matters, OK?" she said as she looked him in the eyes.

"OK," he said, before kissing her on the lips. Noah snored lightly, having fallen asleep in Tray's arms.

Laughing at the sight of Noah drooling on Tray's shoulder Desire said, "I don't know how it is you do it. I've been trying to get him to sleep all day, and here you come to the rescue, where he just collapses into your arms like some damsel in distress and falls asleep."

With a smile on his face he said, "What can I say? I'm what some people need, and some people are what I need. Now, let's get the little one to the car."

After kissing her lightly and going to look for grandma Mabel and Damon, he drove home elated at having taken his life back.

Chapter 21: Surprise, Nigga!

"Nigga, I'm tellin' you, the shit'll work," said Deuce, the hustler that was selling the weight for G-Rock and Philthy.

"Yeah, well, I hope so 'cause I want that nigga Drak since he's the head. You know the saying, 'Cut the head off the snake and the body will die'," G-Rock said as he took a long swig of Jose Cuervo tequila, looking at Deuce with bloodshot eyes.

"Just let me do my thang. I told you, I got everything in place, and it's gonna be a shame because the blow of death is already among them like Judas Iscariot, you feel me?"

$$$$$

Blaze had been in a slight daze since losing Mona. They were tighter than real sisters. Mona had wanted her to be her maid of honor at her and Tray's surprise wedding. Losing Mona had taken a lot out of her.

It seemed like only yesterday that she had been watching the young, seemingly innocent Mona. She'd always had this certain kind of spunk about her that had reminded Blaze a lot of herself growing up in the grimy streets of Brooklyn, New York, alone and lost, but still determined to overcome the obstacles of life that had forced poverty upon her and her siblings, leading her to find a way out for herself. And find a way out, she did.

One day Blaze had spotted Mona coming from Sierra, Nevada, when she noticed a black Firebird was trailing her. Mona kept stopping and engaging in verbal warfare with the man inside, then would return to walking again. Suddenly the car swerved, jumped the curb and cut her off. When the driver jumped out and made an aggressive move toward her, she dropped down into a squatting, balled-up position. At first she looked like she was cowering, then in a flash she swung a straight razor she'd removed from her crotch in a wide arc, slicing him across the cheek. The momentum from the swing spun her in a 360 degree circle, giving her time to snatch the ice pick she used to keep her ponytail up, and stick him several times before breaking out into a full sprint, leaving the guy slumped over the hood of his idling Firebird.

Pulling up on the side of her, Blaze told her, "Get in!" Seeing the look of skepticism on the girl's face she said, "Bitch, you pro'ly killed that nigga. You got blood all over you and I'm your only hope. So, get in and duck down."

Needing no further encouragement, Mona dove through the back window that was rolled down and Blaze burned rubber up off the block. They had went back to the spot, where Blaze got the 411 on this lil gangsta bitch with the innocent face. It didn't take much convincing for Blaze to decide that she wanted her as her off-breed; nor did it take Mona much convincing to accept. From that day forward, they were as tight as ten toes in a cowboy boot. As far as Blaze was concerned, Mona has come into the family having fulfilled her blood oath, but come to find out, she had pain in her soul and violence was a way to find some relief so she wanted no special treatment. If a blood oath was the requirement, then a blood oath she would fulfill. She had dedicated herself wholeheartedly to the MOB $tars, and had proved to be a valuable asset as many men fell victim to her beauty, unaware of the raging hurricane within.

Blaze was suddenly disturbed from her thoughts by the ringing of her phone. Looking at the caller ID, she saw it was Fatima, a friend from out west. "What up, Fatima?" she said.

"Hey, baby girl. Y'all got that reward money on that nigga's head still" she asked excitedly.

"Why, what the deal is?" Blaze asked starting to become irritated.

"Because, I got this bitch-ass nigga in my scope as we speak," she said.

"Where that nigga at?" Blaze snapped. "Don't worry, you'll get paid. I even got a lil somethin' extra for you. Now, where that nigga at?"

"He's at my spot rockin' up two keys of dope right now," she said with a smile on her face.

"Look, we'll be right there. Don't say nothin' to nobody, alright?"

"Alright," Fatima agreed and hung up the phone.

"Good lookin' out shorty," Deuce said, leaning out the passenger window.

"Good bookin' out my ass, nigga! Break bread!" Fatima said.

"Damn, ma! Calm down, I got you. Here," he said as she came around to his side of the Avalanche. As she stuck her hand out, she realized the look on his face, and before she could turn and run, he shot her in the face – POW! – - and once she fell, he shot her three more times – POW! POW! POW! As he looked down at her, he smiled and said, "Don't smoke that all at once, that shit'll kill you."

When G-Rock drove off, the two started to laugh as they fired up another blunt.

After calling Drak and informing him of what she'd found out, she hung up and called Villian, Lil Tech, Mack, Roxy, Cripani and Trigga Dave, who'd all been back in Stockton since Mona's funeral. She gave them all the rundown and everything was set in motion. Just as everyone was getting in the car, Drak pulled up and checked to see if everybody understood their positions. Suddenly, Lil Tech hopped out and told Drak, "I need to holla at you for a minute."

"Do it have to be now, lil homie? We got work to put in."

"I know. Let me ride with you while we holla," he said. "It's important, big homie," he added.

"Fuck it, come on. But I'm droppin' you off around the corner from the hot spot," Drak said as Lil Tech jumped in. "Now, what's goin' on?"

"Big homie, I got a weird feeling about this nigga Tray just being able to walk away without any repercussions. That nigga know too much of the bidness," Lil Tech said while fumbling with his phone. "And don't you think it's kinda weird that Tray just so happened to be out of town when Mona got hit? Then he starts wolfin' this ol' killa shit when he first finds out, but when he pops back up later he don't want no revenge? Why not? 'Cause he been all up under the bitch's ass he was with the night the shit happened. Now he on some ol' forgive my sins shit? I say we knock that nigga's shit in -- straight up!" he said amped up. "Matter of fact, let me call Villian." After dialing: "'Ey homie, y'all ready? Drak is gonna drop me off right in the back by the payphone. Swoop through and pick me up, we're almost there," he said and hung up while Drak listened to the music.

$$$$$

"Ey, nigga, it's goin' down," Deuce said, hanging up the phone. "Let's roll, y'all. Meet up back by the payphone."

As Blaze drove past Fatima's spot, she didn't see any kind of movement through her drapes. Pulling up to the curb, she pulled out her iPhone 6, called Villian and told him what she saw. He told her to sit tight, he had a plan.

110

As little David came walking up towards Villian, Villian said, "Hey, lil man; you wanna make twenty dollars?"

"Ey, man, I ain't on no faggot shit," David said, attempting to be brave.

"Lil nigga, ain't nobody on no ol' gay shit, nigga; I need you to do something for me," Villian snapped.

"Alright. What I gotta do?" he asked with his hand out waiting to be paid.

As David knocked on the door, he thought of all the candy he was going to buy.

$$$$$

"Hey, Drak, pull up to the phone booth, Villian's gonna swoop me right there," Lil Tech said, hitting buttons on his phone, when suddenly Drak's door was snatched open, and before his mind could register what was going on, he was hammered in the face twice with the ass of the assault rifle. Lil Tech snatched the keys out the ignition and ducked out the door. As he laughed and spun around, he held the keys up and dangled them at Drak: "Surprise, nigga!"

$$$$$

After knocking for five minutes, they called David away from Fatima's door. "Thanks, lil man; here," Villian said, giving him another $20.00.

"Wow! Man, big homie," he said and took of up the block.

"Man, something is funny about this. She wouldn't just --"

Blaze was cut off when the night suddenly lit up and quick bursts from assault rifles shattered the silence. As the crew was caught off guard, their natural reflexes caused them to duck. But as quickly as the bursts had started, they stopped, and in the distance tires could be heard squealing as the rubber tried to grip the pavement. Out of nowhere, three cars came flying from behind the apartments: a burnt orange Chrysler 300C; a maroon Z-28 with the roof off, two niggas sitting on top of the back seat, both wearing bulletproof vests and Jason masks; and last was a brown Avalanche with Louis Vuitton paint. All of the thugs brandished assault rifles in the air.

Chapter 22: Betrayed

As Tray was driving Grandma Mabel and Damon home so he could go spend the night with Desire, they suddenly spotted several police cars and fire engines heading down Monte Diablo, towards the rest emergency response team. Thinking nothing of it, he continued on toward his destination.

$$$$$

After the crew spotted the three cars leaving, an eerie feeling came over them as they all looked around one another in confusion.

Suddenly Mack said, "Let's go see what happened back there."

As Villian jumped in the whip and followed the crew, he couldn't help but wonder if his eyes were playing tricks on him, because in a glance it had looked like Lil Tech in the passenger seat of the Chrysler when it had passed by them.

When they got to the back, they spotted Drak's Challenger riddled with bullet holes as he laid slumped over the steering wheel with what seemed to be cocaine dumped all over him. Written in bright red on one side of his car read, "Leader of the MOB $tars." On the other side read, "Dirty cop! Rest in piss!" The scent of cordite permeated the air and mixed with the scent of Drak's blood.

As Villian felt the anguish one only feels from losing someone that you greatly respect, he felt a tear drip down his face. After quickly wiping it away, he said to everyone, "Let's bounce before the police gets here," as he snatched up the MOB $tars' emblem from the roof of the car that was no doubt the ultimate slap in the face by Lil Tech. How could he flip the script on us like that? We were his family! Could he have been sent to be an infiltrator from the start? Villian was thoroughly confused. He felt betrayed and vowed to get answers. And answers he would get, by choice or by force!

$$$$$

After dropping Grandma Mabel and Damon off at home, Tray called Desire who said she was in the mood for some Chinese food, so he decided to go by the Panda Express to get them something to eat. After placing his order, he stepped outside to take a couple puffs off his Black & Mild cigar. Just as he was about to step back inside, he spotted a burnt orange Chrysler 300 C bend the corner with Lil Tech in the passenger seat. As he saw him dip down and come back up with a finger to his nose, Tray realized he was snorting coke. Well, he was no longer Tray's responsibility, so he went back inside to pick up his order as the thought of seeing Lil Tech drifted to the back of his mind.

"Lil nigga, you did that!" Deuce said, giving his nephew Lil Tech some dap before passing him the CD case with the pile of powdered coke piled on it.

After snorting a thick line he said, "I told you niggas I could make it happen. Them stupid muthafuckas thought I was a straight-up muthafuckin' MOB $tar soldier. You should've seen those bitches -- 'MOB! As one!'" he said,

114

mocking the crew he'd deceived. As he snorted another line, he sat and thought about how he'd played the MOB. Villian had truly started to become close to him and he'd definitely be missed. Blaze had been like a big sister, even though he secretly wanted a piece of the Puerto Rican pussy. The rest of them, however, he never did really like. He just played the role so they'd become comfortable with him. Form the time he infiltrated the MOB $tars, he had one mission in mind: to set up Drak for uncle Deuce. He couldn't help but wonder if his traitorous actions would bring consequences banging at his back door as he snorted another line. And for the first time he wondered if he was really ready for the wrath that he'd certainly unleashed onto himself.

Cuddled up next to Tray with Noah's head on her lap, Desire enjoyed what was left of her Mongolian beef and stir-fried rice.

"Damn, baby, that shit was the bomb," she said, kissing his cheek and wiping the grease she'd left behind.

"Baby, you're the bomb!" he responded and kissed her on the mouth gently. "Now that you've eaten, let me put something in your stomach, lil mama," he added with a smirk on his face.

Elbowing him in the ribs playfully she said, "You're so nasty," as she giggled.

"And you love every bit of it," he said as he started to laugh with her. They suddenly shared a passionate kiss, then snuck upstairs for a little more privacy as Noah snored on the couch, oblivious to their departure.

$$$$$

"I'm tellin' you, I seen that bitch-ass nigga in that orange 300. I don't know what's goin' on, 'cause that nigga didn't seem to be in distress. Plus, why didn't they air that nigga out along with Drak? That nigga played us, I feel it," Villian said as he paced back and forth with his fists clenched tight as Blaze and Cripani continued to try and calm him down.

"Baby, we are trying to find out what went down. Come to find out, they found Fatima's body down the block from where we found Drak, at the other payphone. So we believe somebody used Fatima to set us up," Blaze said.

"But that doesn't explain why Lil Tech left with those cats," he said, when suddenly a disturbing thought hit him. "Unless he was in on the setup." Villian began thinking about how Lil Tech had been acting lately: always talking secretively on the phone or texting; always asking about Drak being a cop; his various outbursts; and finally him jumping out the car and needing to talk and ride with Drak at the last minute. As he added all the deceptive components together, a picture began to appear, and it was as clear as if Picasso had painted it himself; Lil Tech was Judas Iscariot reincarnated.

After awaking refreshed but sore from a long night of ravishing love making, Desire jumped in the shower and enjoyed the invigorating effects that it was having on her body. After what seemed like an hour, she emerged feeling like a new woman. When she looked over at Tray, she noticed Noah had found his way into the bed and was curled up next to him with an arm slung over Tray's chest; something he'd only done with Bango.

Deciding not to wake either of them up, she went to make some breakfast. Noticing they were out of eggs and sausage, she decided to run out and grab a few items because they would be at the hospital most the day. As she dashed into the room, she grabbed Tray's keys and headed out the door. While she searched for a CD to play, she thought to herself how beautiful it was outside and how good it felt to experience peace again now that Tray was back in her and Noah's lives. Putting in the T.I. CD Paper Trail, she pulled off with the music taking her to another world; oblivious to the orange 300 that had passed her and busted a U-turn.

"Aw, shit, blood! There that nigga go! Turn around and follow that Cadillac," Lil Tech said after spotting Tray's CTS. "'Ey, nigga, I'm 'bout to knock this nigga's shit in," he added while snorting another line off the CD case in his uncle's lap. He laid the passenger seat all the way back, climbed into the back seat, then said to Deuce, "Pull up on the side of this nigga." Then he snatched the Mac-11 from under the driver's seat, rolled down the window and waited.

$$\$\$\$\$\$$$

Desire expertly maneuvered the CTS as she fired up half a blunt from the ashtray, singing along to the T.I. song: "Oh! I've been travelin' down this road so long, tryin' to find my way back home, the old me..." As she made a stop at the stoplight, she spotted an orange car racing up on the side of her. When she turned to see what was going on, she realized it was too late. All of a sudden she recognized the muzzle of the machine gun hanging out the window as the Mac-11 sprayed a deadly flurry of bullets that punctured her body with severe velocity from the waist up. Suddenly her head was snapped sideways, shattering the driver's-door window as the Rhino slug smashed through her skull, causing it to rock back before finally resting on the steering wheel. Smoke from the weed escaped her nostrils, along with her last breath. The tires hollered as they tried to grip the concrete, but when they caught traction, the 300 C shot off around the corner into a half spin before correcting and squatting off down California Street, heading toward the highway.

As Desire lay slumped against the steering wheel with blood and smoke coming from her mouth, a lone drop of blood fell on top of her shiny platinum promise ring.

"...The old me's dead and gone, dead and gone..." The song continued to play as she died alone and confused.

117

Chapter 23: Death Becomes You

After drinking three cans of 4 Loco, Villian decided to head back to Cal Park Liquors to get a fifth of Hennessey. Just as he jumped the back fence, he spotted a commotion coming from drown the street. As he crossed California Street he spotted something that snatched the breath from his lungs: Tray's car was on the corner, shot up, and people were gathering around it.

Breaking into a sprint, he rushed over to the car, "Watch out! Get the fuck out the way!" Villian yelled, pushing some fool aside. He tried to open the door to Tray's car but they were locked.

"Some lady is inside," one young kid said.

Having been in a hurry, Villian hadn't looked in the windshield. When he did, he spotted a light-skinned girl laying against the steering wheel. Snatching his phone off his hip, he speed-dialed Tray's number.

As he was awakened by the sound of his phone, Tray looked around and noticed Noah lying on his chest. Gently laying him on the bed, he found his pants and answered the phone: "Hello?"

"'Ey, nigga, where you at!?" Villian yelled into the phone with panic in his voice.

118

"Calm down, bro! What's going on?" Tray snapped, sounding worried.

"Nigga, some bitch is dead in yo' car; that's what's going on!" Villian said hysterically into the phone.

"A bitch is dead... in..." Suddenly he jumped up and searched the house calling Desire's name. Panic filled him to the core. As he walked to the front door, he mumbled repeatedly: "No. No. No, God... don't let it be, God..."

When he looked outside, his heart sank as he realized his car wasn't there. "'Ey, nigga, what did y'all do!?" he yelled accusingly.

"Nigga, what the fuck you mean y'all?" Villian asked.

"Man, all I know is, I walk away from y'all and my whip gets shot up?" he said with a shaky voice.

"On my life, we weren't trippin' on you walkin' away, dog. But, Drak got killed last night out west," Villian said. "And guess who was behind the shit?"

Before Villian could even say it, Tray had a feeling he already knew.

"That snake-ass nigga Lil Tech," Villian said. Then he gave Tray the whole scoop on what he'd figured out as he went to go pick him up.

Within twenty minutes Villian was in front of Desire's house blowing the horn. With Noah in tow, Tray got into the car, sitting Noah in his lap. While they headed to Grandma Mabel's house, Noah asked repeatedly, "Where's my mama, Tray? Can I call my mama, Tray?" It was breaking Tray's heart to ignore him, but he didn't know how to answer.

As they pulled up in front of the house, Damon came down the steps: "What's up, bro?" As he noticed the look on Tray's face he said, "What's wrong?"

"Nothin'. I need you to watch Noah for me; I'll pay you," Tray said as his eyes started to water.

"Naw, bro; I got you." He embraced him and added: "Be careful, Tray."

"I will bro. I love you." As he got back into the car he

heard Noah say, 'Can you take me to see my mama?' as he looked up at Damon.

$$\$\$\$\$\$$

As they rolled through Madison Arms they spotted Bob and Weave Betty. She was a notorious swallower known by all the young dope dealers, many of which she had sprung. But to Tray and Villian, she was a for-sure tool that could be used to dig a grave for Lil Tech; she was his mother and would lead them straight to him.

"Bob and Weave; what up, girl?" Villian asked her.

"Shit, you know me. I'm tryna eat yo' dick up till I hick-up and I'm that bitch that don't need no spit cup," she said, bent over, searching the ground for crumbs of crack.

"You wanna make some money so you can smoke?" he asked.

"Nigga, is you hard of hearin'?" she said as she bounced up, looked him in the eyes and went back to searching the ground. "I'll eat yo' dick up--"

"Naw, I'm way cool on that. I'm tryna do some business with yo' son," Villian said with a look of deceit in his eyes.

"Nigga, I'm Tryna Smoke Some Crack! Pleased to meet you," she said, cracking up at her own joke.

"No; seriously. I'll give you some money to buy you some crack. All you gotta do is text him, tell him you have somebody here selling three Tommy Guns and a Glock 10 with an extended clip and I'll give you $500.00 right now," Villian said.

"Where's the phone at?" she said as she raised up and looked inside the car.

$$\$\$\$\$\$$

As Lil Tech snorted another line of powder he suddenly noticed he'd received a text message. As he read it, he reached over and tapped Deuce on the arm. "Hey, nigga, you think G-Rock wanna buy three tommy guns and a Glock 10 wit' an extender and a beam on it?"

"Hell, yeah, nigga," Deuce said, bending down and snorting a line.

"Nigga, slide through Madison Arms, my moms is waiting for us," he said, leaning back as the coke started to drain down the back of his throat leaving a fresh numbing trail.

$$$$$

"Tray, are you sure you want to do this? You did enough by helping me find out where Bob and Weave stayed. I can handle it from here," Villian said, trying to give Tray an out.

"Naw, I got to avenge Desire's death," Tray said as a tear rolled down his cheek.

"Vengeance is mine, I will repay, says the Lord," Villian said, quoting Roman 12:19.

Suddenly Tray looked over at Villian and said, "But, what about you?"

"You can't save everyone, Tray. Just follow the Lord and let the dead bury their own. Now go; I got somethin' to handle," he said as he spotted the orange 300 pull into the gate. "But, before you go, here," Villian said as he handed Tray his old banger. "Never know, you may need it one day. Karma is a bitch."

"What you gonna have?" Tray asked curiously.

"Nigga, you know I'm on some Al Pacino shit. Say hello to my little friend!" he said as he grabbed the M-60 machine gun from the back.

Before Tray stepped out the car, he gave Villian some love in the form of a brotherly hug and a firm handshake, then got out and walked away.

Getting out the car himself and taking a shortcut through the building, Villian ran in an attempt to trap Lil Tech from getting away.

$$$$$

As soon as Deuce pulled in the gate at Madison Arms projects, Lil Tech immediately picked up on a weird vibe and told Deuce to let him out while he went ahead and parked. Sitting in the car and making more lines of coke as the sound of Jeezy's Recession came out the speakers, he leaned over and snorted a fat rail. The rush of euphoria was so intense, that when he opened his eyes, it was only after a couple seconds that he realized he was face to face with death. As he caught the sight of the M-60 out of his peripheral vision, he tried to talk, but the rush from the powder had his tongue numb and stuck to the roof of his mouth.

"Nigga, you got one chance to save yourself 'cause it ain't you I want, but you better tell me who put the hit on Drak," Villian said through clenched teeth. "Now talk!" he snapped.

"Man, I-I was just driving," Deuce stammered, still trying to shake the effects that the coke was having on him.

"Oh, OK. I get it. You think I won't flat line yo' mark-ass!?" Villian said as he raised his Timberland boot and kicked him in the side of his face.

He was about to murder him when suddenly, while warding off the next blow he screamed, "OK, man! I'll tell you! It was G-Rock in the brown Avalanche. I told him not to fuck wit' y'all, but he wanted Drak dead for robbin' him and Philthy," he said pleadingly.

"Where can I find this nigga?" he asked curiously.

"The nigga stays with this broad named Cristi over on Magnolia. The address is 669, apartment 2. Man, please don't kill me. I promise I won't say nothin'," Deuce said as his eyes suddenly shifted toward something behind Villian. Picking up on it Villlan sprayed Deuce and spun with an agility and skill of a mercenary as he ducked and positioned himself for defense against whatever danger was lurking.

122

"Well, well, well. If it ain't Judas himself," Villian said sarcastically while looking at Lil Tech who had a Mac-11 clutched in his grip and pointed at him.

"So, this is what it comes to, huh?" asked Lil Tech with a look of regret in his eyes.

"Bruh, you tell me. How could you play us like that, dog? We took you in like family," Villian said with a confused look on his face.

"It's business; nothin' personal. Yo' man Drak was a dirty pig. He was the enemy in hood clothing, and after he used you niggas up, he was gonna get rid of y'all one by one 'cause y'all knew too much. Y'all was just too blind to see it," Lil Tech said, trying to explain his actions. "Besides, that's one less cop we gotta worry about."

"But, see, that's where you're wrong. He wasn't a dirty pig to us. He gave each and every one of us a chance of having the experience of controlling our own life; something many of us never even had. And you took that. And for that, you must pay," he said.

Suddenly there was a blood curdling scream from a lady who spotted Deuce's bloody body inside the car, which startled Villian. That's all the time Lil Tech needed to get off a burst from the Mac-11, which caused Villians legs to crumble underneath him and him drop the M-60 as he clutched his legs in agony.

"My, my, my... What happened to all that talkin', mister philosopher?" he asked, taunting Villian. "Man. And you know what? I really liked you. You just had too much love for that police-ass nigga, Drak. You looked up to that nigga like he was God or somethin'. Well, bitch, who's your God now?" Lil Tech asked. He noticed Villian looking at something behind him, then realized he'd fucked up.

"Nigga, how does it feel to know that death becomes you?" Tray asked as he fired off two shots to the back of Lil Tech's skull. As he fell forward, his face smacked hard against the concrete causing blood to pool and form a red halo around his head.

123

Chapter 24: Debts Fulfilled

After getting Villian to the car and rushing him to U.C. Davis in Sacramento to avoid being in the same city as the shootings, he called Blaze and explained what had happened with them. As they all rushed to the hospital, Tray couldn't help but think how his involvement with Villian had started when he had come to Tray's assistance, which had always made Tray feel indebted to him. But today, he felt that his debt to Villian had been paid in full when he stuck around and was able to come to his assistance when he was at the mercy of Lil Tech. Now Tray felt he could truly close the door on that particular part of his life now, and move on to greener pastures as he allowed God to shape and mold him into his new identity.

$$$$$

It had been two weeks since G-Rock had saw the news report of the double homicide at Madison Arms apartments that had claimed the lives of Deuce and Lil Tech. He was staying under the radar, holed-up with his lil freak Cristi who would do something strange for some change and somethin' mean for some green when it came to sex.

Sitting in the Lazy Boy recliner with a plate of powder on his lap, he watched her run around and get dressed as she prepared for the surprise she'd planned for him. Lifting the plate of powder to his nose and snorting a fat line, he reached for the remote and turned on a porno. The room was immediately filled with loud moaning as Pinky was taking a pounding on the screen. Snorting another line, he laid back and enjoyed the show.

Cristi finally came out the room with a red and black bandanna in her hand and said, "Your surprise is on its way up." Then she went over to him, wrapped the bandanna around his eyes and kissed him gently on the lips. "You might wanna get extra comfy for this," she added as he heard the front door being opened and the sound of a sexy voice coming from the girl who entered.

"Mmm, mmm, mm. I'ma have my way with that," Blaze said with a 50,000 watt stun gun in one hand. And after handing Cristi the $10,000 in hundred dollar bills, Cristi walked out the door leaving Blaze with G-Rock who was oblivious to his impending doom.

"Damn, sexy, you got this shit poppin' up in here, nigga. You got drank, powder, porno; now all you need is..." she said as she reached for his zipper, unzipped him, put him in her mouth until he was nice and wet and added, "a little of this." Then she stuck the stun gun to his length and hit him with 35,000 watts.

"Aaahhhhhhh!" he yelled as his body went rigid, Blaze still having a death grip on his penis.

"Oh, yeah. Let's let the games begin," she said as she hit him with 35,000 more watts. "Aaaaaaahhhh," she mocked, screaming along with him.

$$$$$

"Some people don't realize that God is all they need until God is all they've got. A lot of our daily struggles, we bring

126

upon ourselves by trying to take shortcuts in life because we don't have patience; or, should I say, know how to have patience. See, patience isn't the ability to wait on something; it's an ability to keep a good attitude while you wait on something -- Amen!" said pastor Saffold.

Tray shook his head in agreement as he thought of how he knew various people who fell into that category; himself included. It felt good to get another chance at life.

Suddenly coming down the aisle was a sight he'd prayed for many nights, but still couldn't believe he was seeing as Villian was being led on crutches to be seated by him and his grandma Mabel, Damon, and little Noah, who knew his mommy wasn't coming home and hardly ever left Tray or Damon's side.

As Tray woke Noah up and sat him next to Damon, he stood up and greeted Villian with a hug.

"Welcome, my boy. It's so good to see you step up in here," Tray said to him as he admired his coke white Versace suit, a shark skin belt, hat and shoes.

"Thank you. Can I sit with y'all?" he asked, sounding nervous.

"Of course. Come on, have a seat," he said. While making extra room for him he looked up and thanked God for answering his prayers.

As the pastor continued with his sermon, Villian said a silent prayer of his own, asking God to forgive him for all of his sins, and to take away all the pain behind the murdering, including the assassination of G-Rock.

After getting Cristi to agree to help them set up G-Rock, he ordered Blaze to give her $10,000 and tell her to be gone, which she did. But little did Villian know, she would have done it for free as a way of paying her debt for turning his mom Delores into a crackhead years ago.

As the service was coming to an end, pastor Saffold asked the congregation, "Is there anyone who hasn't accepted Jesus as their personal Lord and Savior?"

Without a second thought, Villian made his way to the

alter and was surrounded by the praise team as they all began to pray for him.

As they were all leaving the church, Noah pointed at the bulletin board and said, "Bye, mama; and bye, grandma Daisy," as pictures of them both were posted in their remembrance.

As Tray reached down and picked Noah up he said to him, "Don't ever forget, I got you. You know why?" he asked, testing him.

"Yeah," he said as he started smiling. "'Cause you love me as much as Jesus!"

They all started laughing at him with admiration in their eyes. After all, he had lost a lot for his age, and not only could he keep a smile on his own face, but the faces of those around him.

The angels will forever keep him guarded from the dangers that await him.

Epilogue

After seeing his closest friend come before the throne, finally asking for the mercy that gracefully awaited him, Tray felt like his life had become somewhat normal again. He took on the responsibility of raising Noah as his own son. To look in his face and his eyes were a constant reminder of the stability that God had placed in his life. See, at times Noah was the spitting image of Bango and Tray was reminded of his constant need of repentance. At others, however, when he looked into Noah's hazel eyes, he saw the look of aspiration and sincerity —a look Desire had in her eyes — he was reminded of the love and forgiveness that awaited you due to God's grace and mercy. Every month he made it a point to take Noah to visit Desire, Bango, and Ms. Daisy at their resting places. Afterward he would visit Mona's.

Villian walked out of church that day, then he and Blaze walked away from the remaining MOB $tars and moved back to Brooklyn, New York. It was time for a change of scenery. They opened up a beauty salon and a recording studio. In no time their businesses were being employed by everybody, from actresses to rap artists. They gave birth to a 10 lbs. 8 ounce baby boy and named him Treyvon. Life had taken on a whole new meaning for them.

Tray stayed in touch with them and was asked to be their baby's godfather. He had already taken the position of Adult Ministry Coordinator at the church; he would gladly be a role model after being such a menace to society, and he vowed to never look back.

BOOK SUMMARIES

THE BEST RESOURCE DIRECTORY FOR PRISONERS, $17.95 & $7.00 S/H: This book has over 1,450 resources for prisoners! Includes: Pen-Pal Companies! Non-Nude Photo Sellers! Free Books and Other Publications! Legal Assistance! Prisoner Advocates! Prisoner Assistants! Correspondence Education! Money-Making Opportunities! Resources for Prison Writers, Poets, Artists, and much, much more! Anything you can think of doing from your prison cell, this book contains the resources to do it!

A GUIDE TO RELAPSE PREVENTION FOR PRISONERS, $15.00 & $5.00 S//H: This book provides the information and guidance that can make a real difference in the preparation of a comprehensive relapse prevention plan. Discover how to meet the parole board's expectation using these proven and practical principles. Included is a blank template and sample relapse prevention plan to assist in your preparation.

CONSPIRACY THEORY, $12.00 & $4.00 S/H: Kokain is an upcoming rapper trying to make a name for himself in the Sacramento, CA underground scene, and Nicki is his girlfriend. One night, in October, Nicki's brother, along with her brother's best friend, go to rob a house of its $100,000 marijuana crop. It goes wrong; shots are fired and a man is killed. Later, as investigators begin closing in on Nicki's brother and his friend, they, along with the help of a few others, create a way to make Kokain take the fall .... The conspiracy begins.

THEE ENEMY OF THE STATE (SPECIAL EDITION), $9.99 & $4.00 S/H: Experience the inspirational journey of a kid who was introduced to the art of rapping in 1993, struggled between his dream of becoming a professional rapper and the reality of the streets, and was finally offered a recording deal in 1999, only to be arrested minutes later and eventually sentenced to life in prison for murder... However, despite his harsh reality, he dedicated himself to hip-hop once again, and with resilience and determination, he sets out to prove he may just be one of the dopest rhyme writers/spitters ever .... At this point, it becomes deeper than rap .... Welcome to a preview of the greatest story you never heard.

LOST ANGELS: $12.00 & $4.00: David Rodrigo was a child who belonged to no world; rejected for his mixed heritage by most of his family and raised by an outcast uncle in the mean streets of East L.A. Chance cast him into a far darker and more devious pit of intrigue that stretched from the barest gutters to the halls of power in the great city. Now, to survive the clash of lethal forces arrayed about him, and to protect those he loves, he has only two allies; his quick wits, and the flashing blade that earned young David the street name, Viper.

LOYALTY AND BETRAYAL, $12.00 & $4.00 S/H: Chunky was an associate of and soldier for the notorious Mexican Mafia -- La Eme. That is, of course, until he was betrayed by those he was most loyal to. Then he vowed to become their worst enemy. And though they've attempted to kill him numerous times, he still to this day is running around making a mockery of their organization .... This is the story of how it all began.

MONEY IZ THE MOTIVE, $12.00 & $4.00 S/H: Like most kids growing up in the hood, Kano has a dream of going from rags to riches. But when his plan to get fast money by robbing the local "mom and pop" shop goes wrong, he quickly finds himself sentenced to serious prison time. Follow Kano as he is schooled to the ways of the game by some of the most respected OGs who ever did it; then is set free and given the resources to put his schooling into action and build the ultimate hood empire...

UNDERWORLD ZILLA, $12.00 & $4.00 S/H: When Talton leaves the West Coast to set up shop in Florida he meets the female version of himself: A drug dealing murderess with psychological issues. A whirlwind of sex, money and murder inevitably ensues and Talton finds himself on the run from the law with nowhere to turn to. When his team from home finds out he's in trouble, they get on a plane heading south...

TO LIVE & DIE IN L.A., $12.00 & $4.00 S/H: It's the summer of 2003. A routine carjacking turns into the come-up of a lifetime when a young cholo from East L.A. accidently intercepts a large heroin shipment. Soon, a number of outlaw groups, including the notorious Mexican Mafia, is hot on his trail.A bloody free-for-all ensues as the deadly cast of characters fight to come out on top. In the end, only one can win. For the rest, it will be game over....

MONEY IZ THE MOTIVE 2, $12.00 & $4.00 S/H: After the murder of a narcotics agent, Kano is forced to shut down his D&C crew and leave Dayton, OH. With no one left to turn to, he calls Candy's West Coast Cuban connection who agrees to relocate him and a few of his goons to the "City of Kings" -- Sacramento, CA, aka Mackramento, Killafornia! Once there, Kano is offered a new set of money-making opportunities and he takes his operation to a whole new level. It doesn't take long, however, for Kano to learn the game is grimy no matter where you go, as he soon experiences a fury of jealousy, hate, deception and greed. In a game where loyalty is scarce and one never truly knows who is friend and who is foe, Kano is faced with the ultimate life or death decisions. Of course, one should expect nothing less when...Money iz the Motive!

MOB$TAR MONEY, $12.00 & $4.00 S/H: After Trey's mother is sent to prison for 75 years to life, he and his little brother are moved from their home in Sacramento, California, to his grand-mother's house in Stockton, California where he is forced to find his way in life and become a man on his own in the city's grimy streets. One day, on his way home from the local corner store, Trey has a rough encounter with the neighborhood bully. Luckily, that's when Tyson, a member of the MOBTAR, a local "get money" gang comes to his aid. The two kids quickly become friends, and it doesn't take long before Trey is embraced into the notorious MOB$TAR money gang, which opens the door to an adventure full of sex, money, murder and mayhem that will change his life forever... You will never guess how this story ends!

BLOCK MONEY, $12.00 & $4.00 S/H: Beast, a young thug from the grimy streets of central Stockton, California lives The Block; breathes The Block; and has committed himself to bleed The Block for all it's worth until his very last breath. Then, one day, he meets Nadia; a stripper at the local club who piques his curiosity with her beauty, quick-witted intellect and rider qualities. The problem? She has a man -- Esco -- a local kingpin with money and power. It doesn't take long, however, before a devious plot is hatched to pull off a heist worth an indeterminable amount of money. Following the acts of treachery, deception and betrayal are twists and turns and a bloody war that will leave you speechless!

THE ART & POWER OF LETTER WRITING FOR PRISONERS; DELUXE EDITION, $16.95 & $5.00 S/H: When locked inside a prison cell, being able to write well is one of the most powerful skills you can have. Some of the most famous and powerful men in the world are known for letters they've written from inside their prison cells, such as: Martin Luther King; Malcolm X; Nelson Mandella; George Jackson; and perhaps the most famous and powerful of all, Apostle Paul, who's letters are in the Bible! The Art and Power of Letter Writting for Prison-ers will show you how to write high-quality personal and business letters. Includes: How to Write Letters Like A Pro! Pen Pal Website Secrets and Strategies! Letter Templates! Over 50 Sample Letters (Love, Legal, Personal, Business, and more)! And a Punctuation Guide!Don't let a prison cell keep you from navigating and networking around the world; increase your power today!

HOW TO HUSTLE AND WIN: SEX, MONEY, MURDER, $15.00 & $5.00 S/H: How To Hu$tle and Win: Sex, Money, Murder edition is the grittiest, underground self-help manual for the 21st century street entrepreneur in print. Never has there been such a book written for today's gangsters, goons and go-getters. This self-help handbook is an absolute must-have for anyone who is actively connected to the streets.

Made in the USA
Middletown, DE
19 February 2021